bordering

gynergy
books

Cover concept and design:
Janet Riopelle

Printed and bound in Canada by:
Imprimerie Gagné Ltée

gynergy books acknowledges the generous support of the Canada Council.

Published by:
gynergy books
P.O. Box 2023
Charlottetown, P.E.I.
Canada, C1A 7N7

Acknowledgements
I would like to thank Lynn Henry, my editor, and everyone at
gynergy for their patience and support.

Canadian Cataloguing in Publication Data

Armstrong, Luanne, 1949-

    Bordering

    ISBN 0-921881-35-5

I. Title.

PS8551.R7638B67 1995   C813'.54   C95-950195-9
PR9199.3.A76B67 1995

This book is for Joan and Sam,
with gratitude for their enduring and boundless
friendship and support.

As well, special thanks to Juanita Meekis for her
fine editing, comfort and good advice, many pots of tea
and, of course, the garden.

Contents

Chapter I

Every January, like a heavy lid, the sky shut down over the valley. Below Louise's house, the bottom of the flat valley turned into a mosaic: squares of yellow stubble flanked by white fields that had been plowed and left to fallow, intersected by the scrawled lines of irrigation ditches and the bent tired lines of gray trees. Mountains ringed the winter-sodden valley in blank blue walls.

Snow weighted down the whole world, the world Louise could see, the world which was the valley. January meant snow, cold and the blue lines of roads which led away — away from her house and into the town where people got on with their lives; and then away from the town itself, with its tidy houses and streets and fenced backyards, and its three blocks of stores; away over the mountains, over passes and through other huddled cold towns; onward to cities and outward to other places. These were places dimly pictured in Louise's imagination, a collage of images culled from other people's lives — too far away, useless to think about.

Louise's faded, two-storey house sat below the road on the brow of a hill, facing east across the valley. A porch ran along the front and wrapped around the south side. An ancient grape vine tied the porch to the roof. There were apple trees, a gray sagging barn and a fence below the house, surrounding the pasture where the horses grazed. Flowers from what was left of her mother's garden had gone wild and, in the spring, lily of the valley, daffodils and hyacinths sprinkled the yard. People sometimes stopped on the road above the house to take pictures. It was all so picturesque.

Louise shifted to bring her feet closer to the fire. Cold seeped through the cracked blue linoelum with its crazy pattern of worn orange flowers. When Louise was home to tend the fire, the old house warmed gradually through the day, but all during the winter, cold continued to lurk in the corners away from the stove no matter how much wood she jammed into it, and to seep up and into and through the floorboards. The walls and windows leaked cold; she layered plastic and sometimes blankets over them, but then the house turned gloomy and tattered, steadily becoming grubbier while Louise, not patiently, waited for spring.

Country life. Here she sat in her vine-covered heritage country house, with her fine horses wandering around outside and an ancient gray tomcat sleeping on the hearth beside the crackling fire. The water hadn't even frozen yet this winter. She had enough hay for another month and the freezer was still full of the roosters she'd slaughtered in the fall. She wouldn't starve, unless she got too sick of boiled chicken and stir-fried broccoli to eat anymore.

Yep, country life was just swell. She'd long ago stopped buying gardening magazines and country anything because they were all written by people from the city with a death wish: move to the country and die of boredom. Like her. Except she'd lived here all her life and should be used to it.

Piss off, you stupid clock, she thought. It ticked — an annoying little tick which she could just barely hear and therefore kept listening for. Ten in the morning. Already. As usual, she'd awakened early. This morning, she'd managed to light the fire, feed the horses and pour the tea, but nothing else had seemed remotely worth doing. Now she was still sitting at the table, looking over the gray and lavendar smoke-hued clouds. Watching and listening, as the red glowing numbers on the clock relentlessly counted the seconds.

She pulled her feet up onto the chair and thought: what meaningful thing are you doing with your life today? What was she doing besides continuing to sit here, wondering what to do next and how to survive now that her last dollar was gone and no job was in sight because the winter was so long that all the tree pruning and farm work was delayed? Nothing was what she was doing. And it seemed that all the bitter choices in her life had narrowed down to this: sitting in the light from the window, looking out over a gray valley, with nothing to do but sit and wonder what force was going to get her up out of the chair and somehow move her forward again.

"Louise," she thought, "you've screwed up royally again."

The situation was simple. No money. No money, no gas. No gas, no ability to move, go to town, look for work that she knew wasn't there but you never knew. Sometime things turned up. Well, no, actually they didn't, but you had to try. If you didn't try, then you gave up. Neither choice was bearable, but one gave the outward appearance of living, which allowed you to keep your pride and keep up your end of the conversation and sometimes fool yourself that something new and good just might happen. She'd get another UIC cheque in two weeks. The last one had vanished when the starting motor had gone on the truck. The UIC cheques were tiny — enough to buy a few groceries, pay the power bill, buy gas and not much more. They never lasted more than a few days. She could survive as long as she did nothing, went nowhere, phoned no one, ate frugally.

No money meant, perhaps, no phone — no paying the two-month-overdue phone bill. No money meant fear and waking at four in the morning, wondering what to do next; it meant she had to do something, stir out of her winter lethargy. But she didn't feel like stirring any more. The same tired struggle went on day after day, week after week, winter after winter. She felt like sitting here, as still and drawn in as the horses, while the house slept around her and only the clock kept its beady vigil.

It wasn't planting season or picking season or pruning season or anything season; just winter time, desperation time, gray time. It wasn't anytime at all except winter — the hang on season, grit your teeth season, check the mail for the UIC cheque season, live out of the freezer season. Call your friends season. It was a bad time to be in this situation, to be so damn broke that she'd even scrounged the change out from under the litter, grease, dust and potato chip wrappers on the truck seat.

"Call your ex-husband season," she said aloud. "Sure."

There was always Steve. Stephen. A name spelled very carefully, with a "ph." A nice man. A classy name for a classy guy. A man who wouldn't even begrudge her the money. He insisted he owed it to her from the sale of their house. A nice name. A nice man. A nice lawyer in a nice small town where everyone was nice to everyone else except to her. She wasn't nice. Not at all.

She was all the sour sad labels she could think of: bitch, harridan, hag, harpy, evil scary woman. She lived alone because she was such a bitch and because of what she had done to Steve. Everyone knew what she had done to Steve, who had been married to her for seven long years and had tried to give her everything and she hadn't been the least bit grateful. *My, my, to think she lived among us all this time,* people said — or so she imagined they said, because, of course, they never said it to her. They never said much of anything to her anymore. *How had he stood it for so long?* they tut-tutted to each other. *Married to her when she was so rude and ungrateful and such a bitch? How could he not have seen it?* Everyone else told everyone else that they had always thought there was something — never quite been able to put their fingers on it. Something not right. And, of course, she wasn't actually from town, but from the boonies, from a farm, from a poor farming family that had always gone their own way and lived their own life and ignored most of what went on around them. And just look where that got them.

No, she really wasn't very nice. Her parties had never quite worked. And she was too big and she read too many books and she never said quite the right things or held the right opinions. She never got her hair cut properly and her clothes weren't right. *She didn't fit, never had,* everyone told everyone. Or maybe they didn't and she only imagined they did. It didn't matter. Because now just look what she had gone and done. She had proved them all right. After all.

Oh, hell, she really did not want to think about this. Usually, when she got into this kind of emotional tangle, she would find some way to distract herself. She would force herself to clean something or fix something, or she would fetch one of the horses from the field, and ride for miles on the logging roads that snaked over the moutains behind the farm. Sometimes, she'd lean over the horse's solid warm shoulders, close her eyes, and rock and rock to the long swaying; and then, sitting up, she'd put the horse into a fast canter, ducking branches and watching for rocks and potholes. The trees would close in around them; deer and wild turkeys and the occasional bear foraged the woods with them. There was her and the horse and the trees and the tangled paths that wove a maze across the mountainside. And there were no people — no carping, bitching mean faces; no restrictions; no boundaries, anywhere — at least, for a while.

But now, she couldn't forget her troubles and just go riding. It was too cold. The fields were covered in snow, the roads in ice. She couldn't go to town and waste what little bit of gas was still in the truck — and what would she do there anyhow? Drink coffee and eat sugary donuts in the small, steamy bakery where everyone else was doing the same thing — waiting for winter to pass? Hope someone might come by and offer her a pile of money and a great job, a job she could stand and one that paid more than minimum wage? There was nothing worthwhile in waiting for that wishful, deluded fantasy. So here she stayed, sitting, listening to the radio spit sound at her.

Seven-and-one-half years married; and now two-and-one-half years separated. Married finally, at twenty-six, when everyone had given up asking or teasing her about boyfriends and had begun steering tactfully around the subject. Just when she was thinking that dead-end jobs were no fun at all and that she ought to be serious about going back to school, she had caught the town's leading bachelor lawyer, in a surprise move that had surprised her as well. For a while, they were happy, beloved of everyone; life was swell. No more worries about money. Instead of going away, she went to night school, taking the few university-level classes the tiny branch office of the nearest college offered — even taking bookkeeping, which bored her silly, and an occasional art class. But, although everything interested her, nothing caught her interest enough to demand that she pursue it further.

They had no children. She couldn't have stood that. When you had children, you were trapped for good. She and Steve had hardly talked about it, but Steve hadn't seemed to mind. She had told him she didn't think she was ready. She didn't tell him that the thought of children froze her breath in panic. She didn't tell him she thought they'd probably be the worst and most selfish parents anyone ever had and it was an act of mercy to not have children. Because she had been so surprised at his initial interest in her, and so certain it would disappear as unexpectedly as it had come, early on she had got into the habit of not telling him things. She didn't lie, but she never said what she really thought, either. She used to wonder how people managed to tell the truth in their relationships. She even thought she ought to try it sometime; but she never did. She didn't think she knew how. It took all of her skills at pretending just to get by. So she hid her thoughts and smiled too much; and was amazed that it worked and went on feeling awkward and trying too hard.

Even on the day she and Stephen were married, she fought panic, fought the urge to run from the church, shedding her gown and flowers like broken armour. She fought it while she smiled and said nice things and ate and drank, her arm through Stephen's, her face aching and stiff. Occasionally, her eyes snagged on her mother and father, who were solemnly going through the ritual of church and friends and family, smiling and shaking hands with people they had known for years, proud of her at last. She had no idea what anyone else in the church thought of her marriage. Except Celeste, who had snorted derisively when Louise had told her about Stephen's proposal and never lost a chance to make savage comments about him. But Celeste had also shown up for the wedding with presents and flowers, and had done up Louise's hair into a million curls and ringlets so that even Louise thought she looked acceptably pretty for once.

Seven years later, the realization had dawned on Louise that she had missed all the chances there were to miss. She lay beside Stephen at night, and counted up her failures: her failure to go to university and finish a degree, her failure to hold onto a decent job, her failure to discipline herself, her failure to get a hard grip on something meaningful and important and make it ring true in her life.

She knew what she liked — what she loved — but it was no use to her. It was lost, gone and foolish in the world's eyes. What she had loved once, before she was grown, was farming, riding horses, helping her Dad prune trees, planting the garden in the spring when the soil was crumbly and rich and smelled of finely shredded secrets. None of these had any importance in the world in which she existed — or in any world she knew about. They had only ever belonged to the world she and her Dad had shared.

In Stephen's world, these kinds of things were set aside for hobbies and spare time, for relaxation. Gardening was a puttering kind thing you did on weekends, just like the neighbours did. Stephen even hired a man to prune their few trees and mow the lawn and rototill and plant their shred of a garden, in spite of Louise's insistence that she liked pruning, mowing, digging, planting.

Louise's mother would come over to visit, on her regular once-a-week trips to town. Wistfully, she would finger the drapes in the living room and look through Louise's cupboards. She urged Louise to shop and greedily took her to stores, her eyes alight, questioning the clerks, looking at dishes, appliances, tablecloths, thick bright towels. Louise, bored but polite, trailed behind, agreeably buying whatever her mother thought she ought to have. The house filled up with things — furniture and dishes and appliances. Coming downstairs in the morning, Louise would have a sudden dizzy sense of dislocation, as if she had wandered absent-mindedly into someone else's kitchen. She put on a pretense of being at ease in the house as she put on her morning smile for Stephen, to go with the coffee she made for them both. After a while, she stopped worrying that he would figure out her fraud, and instead began to feel increasing contempt for his ease at being fooled.

And then, with very little warning, there was the unexpected and unknown madness that caught her like a virus and left her panting and thrashing and terrified of drowning in something she hadn't even known existed. It left her full of delight and finally understanding all the love songs and trashy rainbow sentimentality of the cards in the Pharmasave. She even found herself writing the odd terrible poem. And taking chances, lying to Stephen, coming home too late with feeble excuses, until finally there was no marriage, no big house, no awkward social life and no more reason to try for one — until, finally, there wasn't anyone else at all. Just her. Just the farm where her parents, now dead, had once lived and farmed and brought up their children, and the rambling old house that desperately needed painting, and the fields full of weeds and the tangled apple trees that no one had pruned or looked after for years. And the two horses she and Stephen had bought to try and make her happy, and a half-dead truck she had bought cheap and that needed a new motor and brakes and a lot of other things.

For a little while it was almost okay. She woke up every morning protected by a sense of disbelief. "That was me," she would think. "I did that. How could that have been me? How could I have done that?" Despite her daily drowning in fear at what she had done and what it meant, she hung on desperately to the shreds of what was familiar. She and Stephen still saw each other; she told herself, and him, that they would remain friends. After all, it was a very small town. But gradually the periods between their stiff polite visits got longer and longer. He forgave her, he said on one occasion. At first, she was very glad and grateful for his forgiveness. It was only on the way home afterwards that she was hit with unexpected fury and confusion at the assumption both of them had made — that she was guilty of a crime. They saw each other less and less after that, and finally Louise began to avoid Stephen altogether. She held up her head when she went to town and smiled at people she knew so they couldn't pretend they hadn't seen her. They smiled back and said, too effusively, *let's get together soon*, but they didn't phone and neither did Louise.

She got work as a secretary in a real estate office, from a friend of her parents who still hoped she and Stephen would get back together when they came to their senses. She paid her bills and smiled and never phoned anyone except for a couple of friends who mostly phoned her instead and invited her over and gave her meals and made her laugh, sometimes. Then she came home to the silent house and thought about leaving, thought about getting a job in the city, thought about other

places she could go and things she could do. She signed up for distance
education courses that she never finished. When the job in the real
estate office ended, she turned to odd jobs, orchard work, gardening,
pruning.

On bitter black days, she took down her father's old rifle and looked
at it and put it back. No one would miss her, she thought at those
moments. No one would care at all. No one did care. Bitterness seeped
from her skin, burnt her like acid.

And, for a long while, in the silent evenings, she wrote long sad,
mad letters to Susan which she never mailed. They piled up until one
day, in a fit of rage, she finally burned them. She didn't write anymore,
but it didn't stop her from thinking about what had happened, about
Susan, about what could have been, might have been, different. It
didn't stop her from lying awake at night and staring at the phone across
the room.

Chapter 2

The phone rang abruptly, cutting through the tangle of Louise's remembering like a raucous electric knife. Celeste, probably. It usually was. Celeste: her best friend, endlessly and unswervingly loyal. She had told Louise more than a few times now that the smartest thing she'd ever done was dump Stephen, whatever the reason.

Louise and Celeste had a bond that went back twenty years, through Celeste's pregnancies, the births of her five children, through drunken bitch sessions and shared depressions, through Louise's marriage and subsequent breakup. They'd saved each other's lives in one way or another a number of times. After Louise had left her safe, carefully constructed and maintained life in the town — when she knew she couldn't breathe any longer from panic and fear; when she was sure she was not going to make it — the chaotic normality of Celeste's house had been her life-raft. That, and twenty years of friendship, was something she could depend on.

"Louise, can you come over?" Celeste's voice, usually cheerful, was tight and afraid. Louise knew Celeste so well by now that she caught all the tiny inflections in her voice.

"What's wrong?" she said.

"I can't talk about it on this goddamn party line," Celeste snapped. "Are you coming or not?"

"Five minutes," Louise snapped back. "And there'd better be cookies." When Celeste was in such a state, there was no point in yelling back at her. But she didn't have to be nice about such crappy treatment either.

She plugged the stove full of wood, went outside, and finally got the truck started after struggling with the choke and pouring gas in the carburetor three times. There was a quarter of a tank of gas. Enough for one trip to town and back. Enough for three trips to Celeste's. Enough for two trips to Celeste's and a possibility of barely making it to town. If she got desperate, she could beg gas off Harold, Celeste's husband. But she could only do that, at most, a couple of times without revealing her state of dire poverty. And that, as yet, she was not desperate enough to do.

Celeste lived in a big house filled with kids and dogs and noise and food. It was five miles down another dirt road in the maze of dirt roads that made up the rural pocket neighbourhood in which Louise had been born and raised. The yard between Celeste's house and the road was full of machines: broken tractors, caterpillar parts and four-by-four trucks in various states of disrepair.

Harold was outside under a huge rusty-yellow skidder, lying on his back on the ice, when Louise's truck slid into the yard in a spray of ice and sand. He glided out from under the skidder, his round cheerfully red face streaked with grease, but, for once, he wasn't smiling. He stared at her like she was some apparition he hadn't expected to see.

"Hiya Harold," she said, but didn't stop. Celeste's voice had been too tight for that. With a grunt, Harold slid back under the truck. When she entered the house, Louise sat in her usual chair and waited for the inevitable coffee. It was as much a ritual as anything else she did, she had done it for so long: clumped into Celeste's house, said hello to the dogs, moved a few cats, kicked aside some toys, sat in the same chair, looked at the magazines and newspapers that were piled high on the table and waited for Celeste to bring forth coffee and cookies.

But today Celeste fiddled with the coffee maker and fooled around getting the cookies for so long Louise knew that, this time, it was really serious. She sighed and waited. Celeste sat down opposite her and stared — anywhere, out the window, at the wall — carefully not looking at Louise.

"Jeezus Christ, Celeste, just say it," Louise said finally. "What can be that awful?"

Celeste looked at her and her face was a staring mask, with two frightened eyes peeping out of red ringed eyeholes.

"It's Celia," she said, and her voice was tinny, flat and far away. "She's been arrested. For drugs. She was carrying drugs across the border and they caught her. She won't say who it was for. She won't say anything. She's up in her room, crying. We were up all night. The police just brought her home. Harold can't deal with it at all. That's why he's outside hiding under that goddamn skidder. I don't know what to do, Lou. I don't even know where to start. I don't know what to say to her. I don't know anything about courts or lawyers. Jeezus, I just don't know. I don't understand this. Any of it. I can't make sense of it."

Celeste's face crumpled but she didn't cry. She slumped in her chair, staring at the table. Louise tried desperately to take in Celeste's words. She'd known Celia all her life — had arrived at the hospital half an hour after she was born, held her, played with her, babysat her, wiped her bum. The kid was as close to being a relative as any kid could get.

"I've tried to talk to her," Celeste said. "She won't even look at me. She's only thirteen, just a kid, a little kid. What the hell is going on? How could this happen?"

Louise looked out the window at the normal winter day. Icicles dripped forlorn bits of water onto the snowdrifts beneath the window. It might clear later, might even begin to warm up a bit. She looked back at Celeste. Celeste's hair hung in spindly drifts around her face. She had pulled a worn pink sweater over her shoulders and she hung onto it with one hand. Her broad shoulders slumped, folded towards her breasts like great sad wings.

"Poor Celia ... how is she doing? I mean, is she coping okay?" Louise said finally, very slowly. The words seemed heavy and useless. She pulled them out one by one, trying to see if they were the right ones. "She must be in shock, or something like shock. God. Police ... arrested ... she's got to be hurt, and bloody scared, I'll bet. Jeezus, she's going to need help to get through this." She paused. No, the words still felt all wrong, awkward. What should she say to her best friend on such an ordinary day that had turned, so suddenly, into something so strange, unlooked for, tinged with foreign horror and the smell of cities and criminals? Celeste didn't seem to be listening to her at all.

"Look, Celeste, honey, you're going to have to pull yourself together for that kid. She needs you a lot right now. Maybe you should think about getting a lawyer, and then maybe get a counsellor ... you could talk to the school counsellor, see if you can find out what's been going on ... maybe talk to some of her friends. I could ask Becky ..." She stopped. Celeste still wasn't listening. She was sitting with her arms wrapped around herself, rocking back and forth. Only the silence got her attention.

"A counsellor ... yes, right. What else? Maybe I should write this down." Celeste got up and wandered into the kitchen, searching distractedly through piles of dishes for paper and a pencil.

When she came back, Louise said patiently, "Your lawyer. Who's your lawyer, Cel? I'm pretty sure you've got to have a lawyer if the police are involved."

"I don't know. I guess we'll ask Stephen. I mean, he's the only lawyer we know. But what do we need a lawyer for? The police have already told us she's guilty." Celeste was making little circles on the paper and then drawing crosses through them.

"Listen, Celeste. Please, just listen to me. I lived with a lawyer. I know a little tiny bit — not much. Don't talk to the police. Please just get a lawyer and let him do the talking. But, come on, don't get Stephen, don't even talk to him, get his partner or someone. Stephen's a nice guy but you know you don't want him around right now. Plus you know each other too well. I mean, for Christ's sake, Cel, you always say you hate his guts. And he doesn't think much of you either. So. Now write it down. Lawyer. L, a, w, y, e, r."

Obediently, Celeste did so.

"Okay, now, counsellors. Talk to the school counsellor. Maybe she knows something about what Celia does at school or who she's hanging around with. Maybe she can recommend someone for Celia to talk to. Although, when I think about it, you're gonna have to go out of town for that. There's no one in town I'd trust to keep their mouth shut."

C-o-u-n-s-e-l-l-o-r, wrote Celeste. Then she threw the pencil down on the table. "I can't do this, Lou," she wailed. "I just can't. I can't handle it. I don't know what to do. I won't be able to go into town ... or walk down the street, or go in a store, without thinking that everyone is staring. Everyone will know ... Oh God, Lou, you've got to help me figure out what to do."

"Look," Louise said, trying too energetically to bring something — a trace of brightness or energy — into the situation. "You can find stuff out, you know. Ask some questions. Somebody must know something helpful — other kids, someone. I mean, a thing like this doesn't just come out of the blue. There's got to be someone behind it. Maybe someone from out of town, probably some Americans. We're so damn close to the border, it's just too convenient for stuff. Maybe we're lucky that nothing like this has ever happened before. Maybe there's someone new in town, something new going on that we haven't heard about. It's such a small place. Someone is bound to know something, right? Celeste?"

Celeste was calmer now, although her face was still white and pinched and dead-looking. "We need coffee," she said. "I can't handle this without coffee." She pushed herself to her feet and went into the kitchen, and then the air seemed to puff out of her in one great blow and she leaned on the kitchen counter, gulping in air in great sobbing desperate whoops, like an animal strangling.

Louise stood up, moved awkwardly into the kitchen and stood beside Celeste. She rubbed her own cold hands on her pants, and then patted Celeste gently, letting her cry until she finally slowed down. Then she put her arms around her and led her back to the table. "Sit," she said. "I'll make the coffee."

As she was rinsing the cups that were stacked around the sink, Harold clumped into the house. Louise was nervous around Harold. She supposed they were friends, but when she visited he often came and went in the house without saying anything at all to her. She didn't know how much he knew about Susan and about her leaving Stephen. She didn't know what Celeste told him.

She and Celeste had never talked about Susan either. It remained an unmentioned, undiscussed, mad chapter in Louise's life — a chapter she had re-read too many times to herself, late at night.

Harold sat down heavily in a chair at the table, and Louise served them all coffee.

"Truck won't start," Harold said sadly. "Battery. Hafta get Al to give me a boost."

"Use my truck," Louise suggested.

"No, that's okay, Lou," said Harold. "Al's coming over anyway, told him I'd weld his busted hitch." He wrapped both hands around the hot coffee cup and held onto it. The three of them were silent.

Louise and Celeste waited, until the silence grew awkward. It seemed impossible to continue to talk in front of Harold. Louise wondered nervously what the parameters were. Did Harold see her visit as interfering in their private family business? Did he want her here? Should she leave? But she was really Celeste's friend. And Celeste had called her here, Celeste needed her. This was women's talk, this knitting together of grief and sharing and concern. Even if Celia was his daughter.

Suddenly, Louise wanted to touch Harold. She had known him her whole life. He used to sit behind her on the school bus. Sometimes, his parents had come over to visit her parents, and they had wandered around outside together. They knew each other but they had never really talked about anything — they just had odd, brief converations about trucks and the weather. She wanted to take his rough grease-smelling hand in hers and hold it until she had managed to console him in some way. But she said nothing. She didn't move. Even more than wanting to console him, she wanted him to go away so she could get on with talking to Celeste — so they could plan, could think this thing out together, like they were used to doing. With Harold there, her place had become ambiguous. This situation was something Celeste and Harold had to face. She had no real place in it, other than the one accorded to her by the bonds of friendship and time. It was awkward, wondering where the boundaries of family privacy were.

So the three of them sat there together in their wintry gloom and, after a while, the talk drifted to familiar things — to the possible coming of spring, the growing of new gardens, the prospect of planting new trees and new flowers, the prospects for broken trucks and ma-chinery trades. There didn't seem to be anything else they could manage to talk about, past their silent grief and fear.

Chapter 3

The truck slid slowly, carelessly, sideways across the frozen, potholed back road, until Louise corrected it and sent it sliding the other way, fishtailing a plume of dust. The road twisted through hayfields and then past lines of spidery gray orchard trees, their branches crooked like witch's hands, pointing stiff watershoots at the sky. In the spring, if it ever came, that would be her work — clipping one jutting, erect, unnecessary branch after another. "Tree haircuts," she called this. Without her help, each tree would eventually choke and strangle in its own rampant growth. She liked the work: standing on the ladder, poking up through the tangled fretwork of branches, the moving clippers steadily shaping the tree into neat, organized growth.

Her father had taught her to prune trees. As a child, she had watched him and followed his gruff muttered orders. She liked watching him work. She liked the slow sureness with which he did things. Often she hadn't understood what he was doing until he was almost through, and then the whole pattern would become clear and she would laugh inside, with delight. He never explained anything; he never said much of anything at all. He said even less in the house, where her mother, bitter at their poverty, held sway and cooked, cleaned, made the rules for their lives, lamented what might have been and never would be — ease, success, the bright happy lives of other people somewhere else, people they didn't know and could only imagine.

Their farm didn't make money but it fed them. They grew a big garden and lots of fruit. All summer and fall, Louise's Mom jammed and canned and froze things. Louise's Dad worked in town — sometimes at the sawmill, sometimes building other people's houses, sometimes in the orchards around the town. In the fall he went hunting and usually shot one elk and a couple of deer, which they ate all winter. He was a handy person. He could do anything, fix anything. People liked him. He was never short of work, but he was always short of money. No matter how hard he worked, the money never went very far.

Louise's mother had been the daughter of the town pharmacist and had never quite reconciled herself to the social comedown of life as the wife of a farmer. But she made do. She constructed her social life out of the Women's Institute and the small country church they all attended. She was a brisk and efficient housewife, and a loving mother to Louise and to Mark, Louise's younger brother. But the bitterness at the heart of her life seeped through and coloured the edges of their moments together, so that even when they were momentarily at ease and relaxed, Louise's mother would say something that would bring back the tension and silence. When they least expected it, she would begin to talk about selling the farm and moving them all into town, where they could go to lessons and groups and a bigger church. She hated the house they lived in. She fought it like a living enemy. She fought it with paint and wallpaper and knickknacks from the catalogue, and she scrubbed and tidied, but the house never responded. Year after year, it sagged a little further on its foundation; smoke from the woodstove darkened the ceiling every winter. Sawdust and mud always littered the floor no matter how many times a day she swept. The only time Louise remembered seeing her mother weeping with rage was when her father had refused to buy yet more paint or linoleum or furniture.

Louise and her father were united in mutual silence before her mother. They worked the farm together, Louise's father labouring stolidly at one task after another. Louise, just as silent and stolid, imitated him, trying to help, learning about gardening and tractors and tools. When they came into the house for food or warmth, they huddled guiltily together under her mother's gaze, unable to admit to themselves that they loved a life she so patently didn't, unable to explain to her — or even put words to — the satisfaction they both felt in the trees standing clean and bare after pruning, in the smell of the earth behind the rototiller, ready for planting, in the sight of the new shoots poking through the ground, in their grunted, almost inaudible conversations about work.

Louise slouched behind her father, imitating his walk, his way of talking, his elliptical sentences, his gruffness. "Goddamn apple trees," her father would say. "No matter how much you prune off that bugger," (meaning the huge Gravenstein that grew in front of the house) "it just grows it back and then some. Take a damn chainsaw to it, one of these days." There was pride in his voice, and also the hidden message that probably Louise hadn't pruned the tree as thoroughly as he himself might have done.

Sometimes, very rarely, when Louise and her father were pruning, they would sing together. Her father would start, singing silly songs, old songs Louise had never heard of, bits of TV commercials, goofy songs. She would sing along and make harmonies. Sometimes they'd yodel, both of them, delighted by the wild sounds issuing from their throats. But they never mentioned these times to anyone, not even to each other.

Louise's brother discovered early on that there was no place for him in this locked family triangle. As soon as Mark could ride his bike, he went to play with the neighbour's kids, and he and his friends soon established a network of bike trails that honeycombed the bush. From bikes he graduated to motorcycles and from motorcycles to cars which belched and roared and muttered from the sagging shed where he and his friends spent most of their time.

Now he lived in the town, married to a pert blond woman who ran his life with brisk efficiency. He had two noisy, rude boys who barely acknowledged their Aunt Louise when she came for dinner. He worked at making cabinets, and his family lived in a new house with new furniture and electric heat. He and his wife dreamed of saving enough money to take the kids to Disneyland. When Louise came over on her rare Sunday dinner visits, she and Mark talked awkwardly about work and the town and friends they used to have in common, and, always, about their parents and the farm. It was their only real bond.

One day, their father had died abruptly of a heart attack. After that, their mother had dwindled into loneliness and fear. She hated living alone, but she struggled on in the old drafty house, making dinner for Mark and his wife on Sundays, or, occasionally, for Stephen and Louise, when Louise could talk Stephen into it. One day, she cut her foot with the axe while chopping kindling for her fire, and never came home from the hospital. Stroke, the uninterested doctor said. Mark had wanted to sell the farm but Louise held out fiercely for keeping it.

Mark's wife, Janet, always tried to talk brightly to Louise about clothes and food. Janet was the manager of a women's clothing store downtown. Louise thought she looked like one of the mannequins in the store — lacquered stiff and brightly painted, stuffed into new clothes and posed in the correct manner. After every visit, Louise swore she wasn't going back. But she did.

"I'm lonely, I'm too lonely," she would think as she drove home to the farmhouse after these visits — drove home to the old cat and the shadowy shape of the horses, head down, caught in the truck headlights as she would turn into the yard.

"I'm lonely, lonely, lonely, goddammit," she would chant out loud to the cat as she fed him. She would turn on the electric blanket, run herself a hot bath in the freezing cold house, and crawl into bed, still damp from the bath.

Once she had said to Celeste, as a joke, that she was so lonely she was thinking of giving her loneliness a name. After all, she lived with it. It crouched in the corner of her house in the evenings, and went to bed with her, and got up with her, and lurked just behind her in the morning while she made coffee, and slithered outside with her while she fed the horses and chopped wood. Celeste didn't get it, though. Loneliness wasn't a word for which her life held any space, not with five kids and Harold.

Now, Louise slowed without stopping and slid out onto the main road leading into town, fishtailing again on the ice and correcting the truck's slide with contemptous grace, one hand on the steering wheel, the other twisted in her hair. The roadside was littered with gas stations and long low buildings that advertised, variously, carpets, linoelum, roofing materials, a livestock auction, furniture upholstering, welding, a flea market, parts for wrecks and wrecks for parts. There were a couple of restaurants that reeked of fried chicken and old grease and had parking lots full of four-by-fours. Gray plumes of exhaust trailed each car down the road. The traffic ploughed the slush into sloppy ruts.

Louise parked outside the bakery. This was her usual first stop when she came to town. The bakery was warm and full of the smell of coffee and yeast and sugar. She quickly checked the room as she came in the door and reassurred herself that there was no one she knew well — no one with whom she would have to make stilted conversation; everyone looked up at her, as well, to see if she was someone they knew. She carefully ignored them, got some tea and a donut and went to a booth. Then she looked around the bakery at her leisure. Everyone in it was someone familiar — not known, but familiar. They hunched in their chairs like refugees: a couple of women with two or three small children each, the children glassy eyed before sugary pastries, their mothers in their faded pastel sweat shirts, smoking and complaining about their husbands; a solitary elderly man, lifting his donut shakily to his mouth, dripping crumbs on his stained shirt; a group of four ladies, dressed to go downtown, sharing the afternoon; a few solitary coffee drinkers, morosely staring out the window; and the same group of old men endlessly dissecting the affairs of the world, deciding what some- one else ought to do, and drinking coffee until their kidneys com- plained and they had enough reason to go home, or go to the bar or the post office or wherever else they could find an excuse to use up their time.

Louise took out a notebook and a pen and made a list. The list didn't amount to much. It said: "(1) Talk to Mark's kids. (2) Talk to Stephen."

She didn't really think there was much she could do to help Celeste — she just felt so lousy about it. Celeste and Harold worked all the time. Harold fixed things, cheerfully helping out his neighbours when he could find time and working frantically when there was work to be had. The payments on his logging truck and on the skidder were ferocious. During the months he didn't work — when the woods were shut down because it was too cold or too hot or too dry or too wet — the lines around his mouth thinned and deepened. He never said anything, though. When there was work, he got up at four or five in the morning, drove thirty or fifty miles in the dark, and worked the skidder or hauled loads of logs to the sawmill, down ten miles of switchbacks and steep grades. He'd make it home in the dark, feed the chickens, say hello to his kids, eat supper and be in bed by eight. If the two older boys had a hockey game, he would go to watch. He would stand with the other fathers at the end of the arena, just behind the glass, against which they pressed their faces like hungry fish. On weekends, he fixed machinery.

Celeste got the kids off to school, cooked, cleaned, did mountains of dishes, drove the kids to appointments and practises and worked at the school in the afternoon as a crossing guard. She crafted embroidery pictures from patterns in her spare time — pictures of flowers and birds and animals — and sold a few of them at the craft shop in the town and at the annual Christmas craft fair. She always nagged to Louise help her with the fair and Louise always refused. Celeste always had ideas for things Louise could do — hobbies she could try, crafts she could learn, groups she could join. Louise always turned her down, and Celeste never lost interest in figuring out what she could try next.

Louise finished her tea and got up, and from habit she stood a moment looking at the notice board by the entrance, with its untidy pencil notes about cars for sale and rabbit meat and "handyman, wants work." Then she went outside, shivering, and walked the two blocks to Stephen's office.

The receptionist was young and blond. "Bimbette" thought Louise viciously to herself. Bimbette ignored Louise. She was a new reception-ist, but the previous woman, who had been older and darker, had also ignored Louise, even when Louise was a legitimate wife with supposed stature and standing in her husband's office.

"Is Stephen in?" she asked.

"Do you have an appointment?" the receptionist returned, without looking at Louise. Instead, she was very busy typing some important paper or other.

"No," said Louise, "I just want to ask Stephen a question."

"I'm sorry, he's very busy right now. Perhaps you could make an appointment and come back some other time."

"Is he in there?" Louise said, patiently. She could feel her face starting to flush. Probably she should just go home and phone him.

"Yes ..."

"Is he with a client?"

"His next appointment is due here any minute."

"Fine," said Louise. "Then I'm not interrupting anything." Quickly, she went for Stephen's door and opened it, but not before she caught the look of contempt on Bimbette's face.

"Louise!" Stephen said, looking up, sounding surprised. He didn't smile and he didn't stand up.

Louise slumped into a chair. She was remembering all over again that talking to Stephen about things like this was usually a waste of time. He didn't like Celeste and he thought Harold was just a redneck logger with the brains to match. She had never been able to explain to him what she saw in them or why they were her friends.

"Hi, Stephen," she said, brightly. She hated the way her voice always got softer and more feminine around Stephen. She'd never been able to make it behave. She even hated the way her body felt. She curled up in the chair and wrapped her arms around her knees; then she uncurled herself, put her feet back on the floor, and tried to look businesslike.

"Stephen, I need to ask you something," she said, carefully. Why was she so nervous? After all, she had been married to this man, slept with him, made his breakfast, seen him unshaven, heard him snoring beside her at night, watched him bleary eyed over the breakfast table.

No actually, that wasn't true. Stephen was many things, but never bleary eyed. Even early in the the morning he was organized, shaved, showered, clean, dressed in a good suit, charging, ready to go, on the phone, handling clients, making deals for people. He was always busy. She remembered admiring and hating that. It made her feel slow and stupid. Beside him, she was slow and stupid. He rarely took time off, except to play golf with other businessmen — men from the Rotary Club. Buying the horses together had been her idea — a silly idea. She had thought that love of the horses was something Stephen might learn to share with her, something from her other life, something she could share with him. It had been just another foolishly hopeful idea.

"You're here about Celeste's and Harold's daughter, I assume," he said. "Lou, I just can't take the case right now. I just don't have the time. Tell them I'll recommend a good lawyer … someone young, just starting out, needs the experience. But the kid will end up in Juvie anyway, its just a matter of time. They should have kept her under control. What the hell were they doing, letting her run wild like that?"

"Stephen, it's not their fault …"

"Well, I always figured their kids would end up wild. But what can you do? Harold's never home and Celeste doesn't seem to care what they do."

"Stephen, they're good caring parents. It's a nice home … and Celia is not going to Juvie … she's just a baby, just a little kid. She can't! Stephen, someone must be behind this, don't you think? I mean, have you ever heard of anything like this … in your work, I mean, has this happened to other kids? Maybe there's someone else involved. I mean, someone older, someone who got her into it."

Stephen looked at her. He was considered, by most women, to be a good-looking man. His eyes were a light blue, surrounded by sandy lashes. His face still tended to freckle slightly in the sun. His blond hair was cut very short. He wore a new dark gray suit and, from across the desk, she caught a faint smell of aftershave. She also caught her own smell of woodsmoke and sweat. Her hair needed cutting. When she looked at her jeans, she saw miniscule flakes of alfalfa still clinging there.

"There's no one else to blame here, Louise. The kid needs to go someplace where she can get counselling, discipline, proper care. She's obviously out of control and it's time her parents realized it. Maybe going to court will finally get it through their heads. Plus the court will order that she get some help. There's no point in you getting involved. There's nothing you can do. The police will make their report, the kid will see a counsellor, they'll make their recommendations and she'll probably be placed in the juvenile detention centre for a while. Then maybe she'll figure out that fooling around with drugs is serious business, and maybe her parents will understand that too. If you can talk them into seeing a family counsellor, then you'll be doing them a favour. Now, if you don't mind, I have a client on his way. Call me later if you still want to talk."

He stood up, and Louise did too. The carpet under her feet was dark blue and soft. She didn't make any noise but she noticed, as she left, tiny flakes of alfalfa and a trace of mud where she had been sitting.

Outside again, the cold hit her. She hated cold. The only time she felt really warm was in midsummer, lying in the sun. She was sick of cold: of being cold, of feeling cold, of fighting the cold. In winter, she felt warm only when she was in bed in the mornings, just before she had to get up in her freezing house and relight the fire for the day.

She had been going to ask Stephen for money — and she hadn't. She had enough gas to make it home, but then she'd have to ask Harold for some gas to come back to town. Which meant she should go to the Canada Employment Centre and check the noticeboard for jobs. There wouldn't be any, but she should do it anyway. Or she could phone Stephen later. She *would* phone him later. Anything was easier than going back in there.

She stood on the gray street, her feet aching in the wet slush, undecided about everything. That's what Susan had said to her — that she was too undecided. She remembered every detail of what Susan had said just before she left.

"Get out of this town, Louise. Make a damn decision. Do something different — anything — with your life. There's nothing left for you here. This is a sad kind of place. It's mean and it's boring because everyone here is always wondering if they couldn't do better somewhere else. Everyone is afraid they've settled for something not quite good enough. And they take it out on each other because it's too small and there's no escape. They take it out on you and you let them. It's no damn good for you. No way can you be free to live any kind of life here. Come with me. We'll travel, have adventures, do crazy things."

But that was just the problem with Susan, she was always doing crazy things — like coming abruptly into Louise's life, tearing it apart with such apparent ease and then leaving, without a backwards glance or an apology. Which, of course, was part of the attraction in the first place — that Susan was so much herself, that she didn't seem to care

what anyone else thought about anything, that she was outside and
free of the small vengeances of the town, the grievances and old feuds
and stale repetitive gossip. Louise thought Susan was amazing. She had
begun by hero-worshipping Susan, and then had fallen in love with
her. It was the last thing, she had thought at the time, that she ever
imagined herself doing. She was so surprised by it — so amazed at the
delirium of her feelings, so perplexed — that she, who had always
been so careful, deliberately and with no forethought at all tore her life
apart.

Susan hadn't stuck around for long. She hated the town, complained about the long gray winter, said loudly that she thought
everyone had collective agoraphobia, that it was like living in a stewpot
with everyone bubbling away in everyone else's business. When she
left, she had asked Louise to come with her.

For hours, Louise had wandered the mountainside above the farm
trying to decide. Could she leave the farm and Celeste and the places
and people she had known all of her life for something unknown,
strange, possibly crazy? Susan was too different. Her life seemed
impossible, unknowable — impossible for Louise. It was different than
life with Stephen, impossibly different. If Louise looked deep into the
heart of that difference, leaving became a wall she couldn't climb,
couldn't see through. She knew that, if she left, she might never be able
to come back. She felt split to the very heart of herself.

And in the end she had said no. She had stayed and Susan had left
— without her, without another word or phone call or letter. And
Louise would never know what might have happened if she had gone.

She would never know because she'd never see Susan again, never
let her see what she'd done with herself or, more to the point, what she
hadn't done.

As she turned on the street, she caught a glimpse of herself in the
silver glass of Stephen's office window. Her long brown hair was
tangled over her worn, torn ski jacket. Bits of insulation were coming
out the elbows. She was wearing sweat pants and running shoes. She
hated looking at herself: too tall; too awkward; big hands; big feet.
Susan had said she loved Louise's hands, turning them over and over,
stroking each finger.

"You have strong hands, farmer hands, warrior hands. I love your
hands," she had laughed. Susan was always saying things like that.
Louise had never known what to say back. Although she had wanted —
and trembled sometimes with the wanting — to say loving things,

crazy things, sexy things. She had no words. Which was why she read the cards at Pharmasave, although that didn't help much. She still couldn't say the words printed on the cards — even after she bought a few of them and hid them in a drawer.

Stephen, too, had said he loved her, when they had first met. She had been amazed that he seemed to mean it. "Do you mean it?" she asked — asked him again and again until he was tired of the question, and sulked and wouldn't answer. Then it was her turn to mollify him, soothe him. She tried to do so without using those words, because she felt so strange saying them. She hadn't any idea what they meant or if they were or could be true.

But she had said it finally, with some relief, to Susan — out loud, and then again and again. She sang it in the truck, bought the whole fairy tale, believed in it; and never questioned whether Susan meant the same thing when she used those same words.

Louise hid her hands in her jacket and went down the street. She might as well go to Mark's place, since she was in town. They'd be surprised to see her, but she might get some lunch and a cup of tea. Mark might not be there, but Janet would be, and maybe the kids would be home for lunch.

When she stopped her battered green truck in front of Mark and Janet's house, her stomach sank. Both of their cars were in the driveway, but a third car was there as well. She didn't recognize it.

Slowly, she got out of the car and approached the house. Janet came to the door, hiding her surprise at seeing Louise under an effusive, gushing welcome. The house, as usual, smelled of furniture polish and cats. The only weird thing about Janet was her passion for cats. She raised Burmese cats, which ran freely around the house and tore the furniture to shreds. There was always a new litter of kittens.

"Come in, Louise," Janet said. "Actually, we were just talking about you. Come and have some lunch. I made a crab salad."

Louise sighed. She hated seafood. And it was too damn cold and gray outside for a salad. Maybe tea: strong black tea, her one addiction.

But Janet had made herb tea. The crab salad sat in little fake crab dishes. There were cloth napkins in napkin rings. Louise was conscious all over again of her messy hair and torn jacket. She hung the jacket by the door and came back into the dining room with its polished plastic furniture. Even though Mark made beautiful wood furniture, Janet ordered hers from the Sears Catalogue. Mark sold his for twice the price.

The other man sitting in the room looked vaguely familiar. He was young and had an air of eager jolliness about him that marked him as some kind of salesman.

"Good that you're here, Lou," said Mark heartily, coming over to give her an awkward kiss on the cheek. Louise stiffened. Mark never did such things. What the hell was going on?

She sat down. Janet poured the minty herb tea, and passed her a plate. She sighed and helped herself. Free food. Not to be sniffed at.

"So, Lou, we were just talking about the old place."

"Yeah?" she said, going absolutely neutral, calm and still. "What about it?" She paid attention to the salad, with its chunky flakes of red and white fish. Not a crab salad. A fake crab salad.

"Well, Janet and I have been meaning to talk to you about it for a while. So we kind of called in Ned here, to get some advice."

"I see," she said. This time it took a careful tensing to keep her voice still. Now she recognized him: Ned Baker; a round, fat, red-faced man; a Pillsbury doughman; a real-estate agent who did property assessments. What else did she know about him? He was reputed to hit his wife. Who had told her that — Celeste, or Becky maybe, or someone else?

"Well, he figures we could get quite a bit out of the place if we subdivided. We could get the timber off it first. That piece above the power line. Lots of yellow pine there. Could just call a contractor, get an estimate. Get someone who'd do a good job, not too much mess — selective logging or whatever. Dad was always going to do that and never got around to it. No point in wasting that timber. Should be harvested, Lou. Worth major bucks, these days."

"Rake off the timber, then sell, is that what you're saying?" she said. This time, she couldn't help it. Her voice had a thin edge, a tiny sharp shred of jaggedness.

"Now, Lou, we didn't figure you'd like it much but you have to look at our side of it. The land is just sitting there going to waste. Not like anyone's farming it or nothing. We could hang on to it for a while longer, I guess, if we get enough out of the timber."

There was silence. Louise took another bite of her salad.

"Jan and I want to build a proper shop downtown, sell new furniture, bring in couple of new lines — crafts and stuff, drapes maybe, good money in drapes. Combine it with my workshop in the back. Could go big. Town's growing. We need some start up capital."

"I use it. I live there. It's my home." She was sorry as soon as she said it. It sounded whiny, pouty, like a child talking — not what she'd meant to say.

"Hell, the damn house is going to fall down around your ears one of these days. Not like you ever do much of anything. Should be painted. The roof needs fixing. You don't even mow the damn lawn."

"Oh, yeah, like you really care. Like you come out and help." Anger flashed, out of control, in her voice. "You know damn well I'm either working or broke. How in hell am I supposed to find time to paint the house? Why don't you buy the paint and do it yourself if you're so worried about it?"

Hearing the anger, both Ned and Janet leapt into the conversation.

Ned, who had probably sat through this kind of conversation before, said brightly, "Now, of course, you have lots of time to talk this over and figure out what will suit you both before you make any kind of decision. No hurry, no hurry at all. I've got to be getting back to the office so you just carry on here and let me know what you decide." Hurriedly, he began picking papers off the table and folding them into his briefcase. He said his goodbyes and dusted out of the house with unseemly haste. Janet saw him out and then came back to the dining room where Mark and Janet were sitting in stony silence, not looking at each other.

"Jeezus, Louise," Mark started, disgusted. "I gotta work in this crapping town, y'know. You might try and act civilized, once in a goddamn while."

Janet's voice came fluting in high tones across the room. "Oh, Louise, did you see the new litter? Seven, and all perfect blue toned. They're just so sweet, I don't know how I can bear to sell them. Come and see when you're finished your lunch."

Louise said, cautiously, "Not to change the subject or anything, but have either of you heard anything about kids and drugs in this town?"

Mark looked at her. "Where the hell have you been lately, Lou? Kids in this town been using drugs since before we were born. Drugs now, drugs then, drugs in the future. Booze, drugs. They all go through it. We did."

Well, some kids, Louise thought privately. Mark had been through it, at least. "Your kids ever say anything much about it?"

"Lou, what the hell? Kids don't talk to their parents. You know that. I ever catch those boys with drugs, I'd whip their butts. But it happens. You know that. What's the big deal?"

"Celeste's kid. Celia. Got caught coming through the border with drugs. I don't understand it. She never seemed the type. I'm just wondering if there's someone else behind it."

"Ah, they never do seem the type. But they all try it." Mark was silent for a long time. Janet had disappeared into the kitchen to do dishes. "Nope, can't say as I've ever heard anything. I'll ask around, I guess. Most I can do. God. Poor Harold, eh."

"Poor Celeste," snapped Louise. "She's the one has to deal with this shit. Harold just hides under his goddamn trucks, sniffing oil or something."

"Yeah, well, it's pretty lousy for everyone. Stupid kids. Well, you know, Lou, whatever I can do ..."

"Thanks," Louise said. They sat there in silence again. The winter light from the window and the yellow light from the chandelier overhead mingled together. Outside the clouds gathered, darkening. It was probably going to snow.

"I better go, Mark. Got stuff to do. You haven't heard of any work happening, eh? Need a few bucks to pay a few bills. Had to have a new starter for the truck."

"Might be green chain work at the mill. You up to that?"

"Done it before," she said. "I'm not that fucking old yet. Anyway, I'm outta here. Say thanks to Janet for lunch."

"And think about the land thing, Lou. We both need money."

Louise sighed. "Yeah, sure. Whatever. See you." She fled out the back door, around the house and into the truck, shivering again and still hungry.

Chapter 4

The conversation with Mark had left Louise shaken. When she got home, the blue winter dusk was settling over the farm. She split a bale of alfalfa and lugged it down to the horses, who were waiting patiently, heads down, at the fence. She split kindling, re-lit the fire, looked into the bare cupboards for anything interesting, and finally settled on rice and instant noodle soup. It was about all she had left. Then she sat down at the table. It had been a long day. The morning's conversation with Celeste seemed very long ago.

What if Mark carried through on his threat to log the farm? Technically, the place belonged to both of them and they were both supposed to agree on anything they did with it. But she supposed that, much as she hated it, Mark was right. She had no money. Even a little money would make a huge difference in her life. There were so many things she could do with it. Fix the truck. Paint the house. Buy some better clothes. Maybe she could take a few more courses that might even prepare her for a real job — not that anyone in the town would hire her.

She and Mark both needed money; they always had. She couldn't remember a time when a need for money hadn't ruled their lives and their parents' lives. So what harm would it do to cut down a few trees? What harm would it do, for that matter, to sell the place, take the money, go to school, move away, live somewhere else — do something, like Susan had told her to do? She could make up for the failures in her life. Money could do that. So could the outward manifestations of money. Clothes. A car. A new car.

What in fact, was she hanging onto here? An old house, mouldering into the hill. A few fields with sagging fences. A garden. Old fruit trees that needed more tending than she gave them. Two horses, some chickens, and a hundred and sixty acres of pine, fir, cedar, and tangled brush. Old trees — decadent trees, they were called. Better to cut them down and give new trees a chance to grow, or so somebody said — somebody, somewhere, who ought to know.

They'd always taken it for granted, having land. It gave them a peculiar arrogance. Louise remembered her mother scheming to persuade her father to sell, seduced by the glitter of the dollars the land would bring. It was worth far more now. The taxes went up every year. It was a strange equation to make, land and money, but one that everyone made. Louise hated it. Land was something you lived on, worked, farmed, walked over, grew to know every waking day of your life, until every fine detail made a difference, until you knew down to the last leaf and twig what time of the year it was and what was growing, what was ripening, what it was time to do. It was yours when every bird call and bird's nest and butterfly and frog and grasshopper was familiar, when whatever you heard, saw, smelled was wonderfully, comfortingly, endlessly familiar; but an unfamiliar sound — a car backfiring, a strange voice, a chicken screeching out of turn — could wake you with a quick adrenaline shot, checking patterns and rhythms to find what was out of place.

Louise tried to see herself somewhere other than here, leading a different life, doing different things. Doing what? That was the problem; that was always the problem. She wasn't that old: thirty seven. She was thirty-seven already ... Half a life gone and she didn't feel she had lived yet. What held her here, chained? She remembered being seven and walking through the orchard with her father, proud that they walked on land they owned, proud to work beside him. If there was a way to make money off the farm, she would have done it already, but she knew better. She'd watched the farms around the town give way to subdivisions. If they sold the farm, what would she have to depend on? Who would she be then?

It was ridiculous to be so damn sentimental. That was one of her main problems. She had never grown up, never dealt realistically with life, never got a decent education, never made anything of herself; she spent her time clinging to a piece of land and stale memories. She wondered what a psychologist would say about her. Something about immaturity, probably. Dependent.

A log exploded in the fire and she jumped. Becky had once said, when they were sitting around a fire somewhere, that logs popping like that were spirits talking. But Becky could say things like that. She was half Cree, or part Cree, or all Cree, depending on how she was feeling and where she'd been lately. Becky was her other best friend, as different from Celeste as she could be. She came and went, worked at itinerant jobs — cooking, treeplanting, waitressing, pruning. She'd been a social worker once, a long time before and not for long. She and Louise had met while they were doing orchard work together.

Louise stood up, yawning. She was tired but she didn't want to go to bed. She slid her jackknife from her pocket and picked up her latest piece of wood from beside the fire. Doodling, she called it. Shaving endless tiny bits of wood, small curls of cedar, from a block, to see what emerged. Sometimes she kept the results; mostly she burned them. The shavings made good kindling. It wasn't something she had ever told anyone about. But it satisfied her hands — to be working while she mulled and worried over her life.

The house creaked and settled around her. Mark had once told her he thought the house was creepy. When they had come out to clean and organize things after their mother's death, they had tiptoed around like children, expecting at every moment to hear one of their parents, to hear the fridge door open, to hear their mother rattling pans from the kitchen.

They had made tea, and, as they sat at the kitchen table, the full realization that their parents were dead and they were adults had hit them. Together, Mark and Louise had sat in silence, while slow tears seeped, unwilled but somehow not embarrassing, from both of them. Then without discussing it, they got up, finished the work of cleaning the house and went home.

The house had sat empty and forlorn until Louise left Stephen and moved back in. Perhaps by then the ghosts had had time to leave. When Louise walked in the door and dropped a box of books on the floor, she merely felt as if she had come home after a long absence. The house had folded itself around her like a lonely friend. She had moved her few things in, brought the horses here, bought some dishes at the auction, scraped together the shreds of her pride and her life, and had begun, grimly, to put it all back together. Celeste and her ready supply of coffee helped a lot; that, and Becky, who understood about Susan.

Susan, who laughed. Susan, who travelled. Susan, who had black hair and brown eyes, and strong hands; who loved horses, cats, dogs, fast cars and whiskey, and didn't seem to care what anyone thought and was as different from Louise, or Stephen or anyone else they knew, as anyone could be. Susan, who had only stayed one year because she came just for work. She made a good living as a computer consultant and she took private contracts so she never stayed in one place for very long. She hadn't stayed in the town for more than a few months when she knew, she said, that it wasn't for her.

"What a mean little bitch of a place," she said one night to Stephen, over dinner at Louise and Stephen's place. "Don't people here ever celebrate, ever just get happy, feel joyful, feel loving? Life is supposed to be about having a good time, at least once in a while. All they seem to do is run each other down, chase each other's wives or get drunk."

Stephen was offended. "We're not a trendy place," he said, stiffly. "We're a very quiet, very traditional small town. But we love it here. We're a very contented community. People can depend on each other."

But Susan had stared at him thoughtfully. "I've lived in lots of small towns," she said, "and none of them are ever the same. I can't quite figure it out, maybe its the weather or the geography, who happens to live there, or something. The history. Where people came from. They're all different. But what I can't figure out is why this is such a sad town. People here hurt one another. Nobody hangs together much. Maybe for a while and then the next thing I know they're gossiping all over town about someone I thought was their best friend."

But Stephen wasn't mollified. "I daresay we're not much different from any other town this size. We're a quiet place. We have lots of retired people. People tend to stay here. They may not have much education but at least they know where they belong and what's important in life. The people who are here like it here. They can have a good life, a sane life. People here are normal." He smirked, just a little, on the last word, and Louise stiffened in her chair.

Louise wasn't sure what Stephen was referring to, but she had heard it before in connection with Susan. She'd put it down as a reference to her lifestyle, her city clothes in their fuschias, jet blacks and purples, her dangling earrings and short-cropped, black hair.

Despite his smirking, Stephen actually seemed to like Susan; liked arguing with her, liked the fact that she smoked and swore and stretched her long legs under his table and argued about business and the economy and politics. Susan seemed to like Stephen, too. For a while, Louise wondered if she was supposed to be jealous. She wasn't. She couldn't imagine being jealous of Susan. She was too glad that Susan came over at all, that Susan brightened her life by coming in the

afternoons to drink coffee and joke and tell stories. Shyly, she invited
Susan to go riding with her, and wasn't surprised to learn that Susan had
ridden all her life, that she had won prizes, that she loved horses too.

She got brave enough one day to ask Susan about relationships,
about her past. They were sitting under a massive yellow pine which
had split open the granite face of the mountain and mantled it with
years and years of pine needles.

"Yeah, I had a husband once. Great guy. I really liked him. But,"
and she turned to Louise with an odd grin, "then one day I up and left
him for another woman. Poor guy. He never really got over it. I think
he's married again now. I haven't seen him for a while."

Louise spliced some pine needles together. It was a habit, something she'd learned to do from learning to braid and splice leather. Her
hands always needed to be busy doing something — working or carving. They were big hands inherited from her father. She noticed how
brown and wrinkled they were, holding the thin brown threads of
needles together. Then it occurred to her that Susan was waiting for her
to say something, that she'd trusted her with a confidence.

"I guess I just never thought about it," she said finally. "I mean,
other women. Around here, no one ever thinks about it."

"Oh, sure they do," Susan said softly. "They just never talk about
it, you mean. I know at least four gay men in that town already."

"Really?" said Louise. "Who?" Then she immediately felt stupid. "I
mean, you don't have to tell me, I'm sorry, I shouldn't have asked."

"No, I'm not going to tell you," Susan said, looking at her. "It's not
my place." She stared across the valley. Maybe she was going to say
something more. But then she laughed and jumped to her feet. "Anyway, now you know the big secret. It's true. I'm not normal. Poor
Stephen. I think he's figured that out by now. C'mon, let's get back.
Horses'll be cooled out by now."

All of which left Louise thinking with complete bewilderment and
amazement about this new possibility that had always been there, that
she must have heard about in the papers and on the radio and from
other people, and never thought about. She remembered Mark talking
about two women who had moved to town and started a small art
gallery. They lived together. "Lezzies," he had sneered. She had
laughed with him, she remembered, now feeling stupid. The women
hadn't stayed more than a couple of years.

So, it was true about Susan. She hadn't believed it because the
possibility had never entered her head. She'd just never thought about

it. It was a city thing, something no one ever talked about. Another woman. How peculiar that must be. But free somehow. Sex with Stephen was pleasant. Not what she had expected when she got married. Her previous encounters with boys and men had been hasty, hurried, something to put up with. But she discovered, with Stephen, that her body liked sex, demanded it sometimes, even though most of the time she was left feeling restless, feeling she had gotten close to something, but never close enough. Some nights she craved the contact, the warmth and touching in the brief interlude before sleeping. She liked it best when she could initiate sex, when Stephen waited for her, and she could push at him, get him to move, get him to wake up and then leave him panting, sweating and, finally, asleep. She told herself that she was satisfied when he was. Then she could dream in peace.

Another woman.

It became impossible to be at ease with Susan after that. There was a crack in their friendship — an edge, sometimes sharp, sometimes warm and glowing, like cut steel. Louise first began to suspect that Susan was flirting with her after the birthday party she held for Susan. Several other couples had come, and a few single women, but only Susan had stayed late after everyone else had left, until even Stephen gave up and went to bed and there were just the two of them, drinking the bits of leftover wine from the bottles in the kitchen and laughing and laughing and laughing. Everything they said seemed rich and witty; the kitchen was warm and redolent with laughter and light. Louise had turned the lights out and littered the kitchen with candles, like a scene from a foolish movie. The candles dripped and glowed.

Finally, Susan had left. They hugged at the door. Susan kissed Louise on the mouth and the shock of her lips woke Louise up. Hastily, she disengaged herself, said good night and went straight upstairs to bed. She curled herself against Stephen's solid warm back. The house sighed and settled around her. She wriggled her hips down into the slight hollow in the middle of the huge bed; the streetlight shone steadily in the window. She closed her eyes.

The feel of Susan hovered around the edges of her mind like perfume; the feel of Susan's lips. They kissed her over and over. She went to sleep still feeling Susan's lips, warm and round and sticky with wine, on hers. She went to sleep, smiling a little to herself. Susan had said she was coming by in the late afternoon to go riding. Whatever it meant, she would see Susan again.

Chapter 5

When Louise woke the next morning, her first thought was for Celia and her second for Celeste. Her house seemed even colder than normal. She propped herself on one elbow and sighed. The yard was a mist of white snow and snow was still falling; the mountains across the valley were only a memory. It was a good day to stay home; a good day to stay in bed. But Celeste must still be in a state, she thought. She'd better phone when she'd had time to wake up — maybe after her first groggy sip of tea, after the fire was going and the house was starting to warm up.

She dressed as fast as she could, split kindling, lit the fire, waded through the thick snow to the horses, broke open a bale of alfalfa and spread half of it on the snow, then came back to the house to make tea. The phone rang. Celeste, already. Louise sighed.

"I can't come over, Celeste," she said. "I'm out of gas and money. I've got to phone Stephen this morning. I've got to do something about my life." But Celeste wasn't having any of it.

"I'll pick you up," she said. "I'm on my way to the school. I'm doing what you said. I've got appointments with everyone — counsellors, the principal, I don't know who-all the hell I've talked to. And I can't go there by myself. You've got to come with me. Get dressed. And put the goddamn coffee on."

Celeste's heavy car skidded into the yard and slid to a stop. She stomped into the house, shedding snow, scarves, mittens and boots.

"Jeezus H. Bloody Christ," she said. "Just what we need. More bloody snow. More bloody winter! One of these days, I'm going to drag

Harold away from here for the winter. Maybe we'll take one of his stupid trucks and load all the kids and animals on it and go to goddamn Disney World. Wouldn't that be a sight?" She tried to laugh, but it came out as a long snort. She sank heavily into a chair, while Louise fetched the coffee. They stared at each other.

"How ya doing, Cel? How's Celia?"

"She won't talk to me or anyone, just lays on her bed, crying, and when she's not crying, she's mad at me. I asked her if she'd go to a counsellor, and she wouldn't say anything. She snuck downstairs and phoned someone, and when I asked her who it was, she hung up and marched back to her room and slammed the door. Kids! Jeezus! Why didn't someone warn me?"

Louise looked at her. "Someone's got to know something. Maybe this counsellor person has got some brains. At least, she'll know who Celia hangs out with, who she might be phoning, what's going on at school."

"Oh, I already know her friends. They're okay kids. Hang around the 7-11. Smoke a bit too much, but they're over at the house all the time. They're okay. Nice kids. I know them."

"Cel, c'mon. They can't be all that nice. Do they do dope? Or do you know? Your problem is you always think everyone is nice. People aren't nice. They're not kind. And mostly they don't give a shit."

"Oh, c'mon now Louise, you figure just because a few people have treated you bad the whole valley is rotten, but it's not true. People are just people. They're mostly all the same. Some make mistakes, do a few rotten things, but you have to give them a chance. You shove people away before you even know what they think. This is a good place and someday you'll figure that out when you get over being so damn prickly and defensive."

It was an old argument. They continued it while they struggled into layers of clothes, got into the the car and out of the yard.

"I'm not prickly," Louise complained. "Get it straight, will you. I'm a fallen woman, a scarlet Jezebel, and you know it."

"Jeezus, Lou, nobody cares why you left Stephen. Most people figure you got tired of him and left. And who could blame you for that? Anyone with half an eye could see you were a mismatch from the word go. Besides, people got other things to worry about. It's all water under the bridge."

The dry snow billowed up from under the car wheels; they drove in a cloud, barely able to see the road ahead of them. Louise huddled into her coat. It was too cold. Her feet hurt. At this time of year, it was impossible to believe the cold would ever end, that heat would come back into the earth — such heat that one could sit outdoors, lie in the grass with no clothes, welcome the touch of cool water, watch flowers nod over the warm grass. She couldn't even imagine it.

Once she and Susan had made love outside on the grass. It was Susan's idea. Louise had been afraid and managed to say so. They were up on the mountain, lying together on a blanket laid over the pine needles, the horses tied, the sun shining on white clouds and a picnic basket. Like something from a story or a Hallmark card.

At first Louise had been stiff and unwilling; but, finally, she had been so overwhelmed by the setting, by the care Susan had taken to bring her here and make her feel safe, by love and need and lust, that she had stopped being self-conscious and worrying about someone seeing them, and had let herself go, let a tidal wave of love and fierce pain and desperation sweep out of her into the shimmering tendrils and leaves and blue butterflies fluttering up into the emerald sky, until she was crying and laughing at the same time, and then just crying and crying, and not even sure why.

When she had come back to herself, Susan was lying on one elbow, watching her and smiling. Louise had opened her eyes and Susan had very carefully kissed each of Louise's fingers, one by one, and then rolled away and got dressed, still smiling, without saying a word. She had left Louise on the blanket, wondering. She hadn't cried in years, not since her mother and father had died. And not even then, not really.

Come to think of it, she and Susan had never really talked after that. And why, Louise was asking herself now — not for the first time — why had Susan just got up and left her like that, lying there with salt flaking and drying on her face? She had never asked Susan and she had never understood. Instead, she had sulked, felt hurt, shrunk back into herself, pulled in the tendrils of trust and love; she got up and rode back home with Susan, pretending to be in love and happy, and had gone back into her house and cried some more.

That evening, she had told Stephen about the the whole thing. His first reaction was one of disbelief; then he said, tolerantly, as if to a small wayward child, "Well, take your time, maybe this is just something you need to figure out." So she went on living with Stephen. The only difference was that she moved into the guest room. She went on making coffee in the morning, and buying groceries and vacuuming the rug and reading books in the long afternoons, when both Susan and Stephen were somewhere else.

But when she thought about it later, she realized that was when something changed. The next time Susan called, there was an edge between them that didn't disappear. Louise figured bitterly that when she had stopped lying, she had lost both of them.

"So it goes," she thought. She shrugged her shoulders inside her coat and then glanced at Celeste. Celeste was driving as if her life depended on it, both hands on the wheel, staring at the tornado clouds of snow billowing up from the wheels of their car and the other cars and blowing across the road in sudden hysterical gusts.

She turned and looked at Louise. "You might have to carry me in there," she said, "but just don't let me talk us out of it, alright?"

Louise nodded.

" I hate this," Celeste mumbled. "I just hate this."

"Just hang on, Celeste," Louise said. "We'll get through this. It's going to be okay." The words were not adequate, not even barely, but they were all she had.

The counsellor's office was warm, even stuffy. There was a desk covered with paper, a few books, two orange plastic chairs, a framed, terrible painting of mountains and a foaming creek with birch trees. They waited, stiffly upright on the hard chairs. The counsellor made a brisk entrance — tall and blonde and very professional. She didn't wait for an explanation or ask any questions, simply strode in, introduced herself and shook hands, barely glancing at them. As soon as she sat down, she began speaking. She already had Celia's file on her desk. She picked it up and held it in her hand as she spoke.

"Your daughter," she said to Celeste, ignoring Louise, "is doing reasonably well in school. Her marks are average. Until recently, we have considered that she has been working to her potential. Any trouble at home, any changes in the home that we should know about?" She peered at Celeste, who shook her head.

"Fine. Lately, her marks have been dropping off slightly. We've also had a few incidents of skipping school. We're you aware of this?" Mute, Celeste could only shake her head again.

"No? Fine. Well, we'll continue to monitor her situation; it may be necessary to schedule a session with her. I have discussed your daughter's situation with a counsellor from the Mental Health Facility, and he doesn't feel at the moment that there is a need for active intervention. However, as I say, we will continue to monitor. Now, was there anything else you wished to discuss with me?" She paused, smiled. Celeste struggled, couldn't get the words out and stopped.

"Fine. Well, thank you very much for coming in. Always nice when parents take an interest in their children's progress." She smiled.

"Wait," Louise said. Celeste and the counsellor both stared at her.

"Excuse me," the counsellor said. "And you are … ?"

"Louise McDonald," she mumbled.

"And your relationship to the child … ?"

"Well, I guess, I mean, Celeste asked to me come for support, to just be with her, and, well, what I'd like to say is I've known Celia her whole life and I'd just like to ask a few questions."

"I'm sorry," the counsellor said. "We only discuss these kind of situations with the immediate family. I have another appointment now. Perhaps if you'd like to come back some other time …"

"Wait," said Louise. She thought to herself that her voice sounded whiny. She felt stupider and stupider. It was hard to phrase the words. Her tongue was stuck inside her mouth and didn't want to move properly. "I just wanted to know, I mean, what exactly do you mean by monitor? How do you monitor? You talk to these kids or what? And what do you mean by intervention? What intervention? What are you talking about."

The counsellor took a long slow breath. She frowned at the wall, said everything with painstaking clarity. "When we encounter a situation in which one of our young people is acting out, or becoming dysfunctional within the school community, we try to assess and monitor the situation, and, if necessary, we intervene before it gets out of hand; either we call the student in for counselling, or we schedule a conference with the family so we can all share the pertinent information."

"But what is intervene … I mean, what do you do?"

"We do an assessment of the situation, call together the appropriate team members and evaluate what needs to be done, and then make a decision."

The counsellor stood up. "Now, if you don't mind …"

Louise gave up. But coming out of the school, she exploded at Celeste. "Jeezus, what a bitch. I guess she thought we were just a couple of idiots who don't understand English."

"Oh, c'mon Lou. She was just doing her job. I thought she was nice. I mean, she knew who Celia was, she's been paying attention to her behaviour. Isn't that what she's supposed to do?"

"Doing her job, sure, if that's what you call it. But she didn't really say anything. If you listened to her, she basically said she wasn't going to do anything. She didn't even seem to think this was a crisis. They've got kids getting arrested every day, or what? And I thought we were going to talk to the principal."

Celeste looked confused. "He was supposed to come to the meeting. I guess he was busy or something."

"Okay, so now what do we do? Just go home?"

"No, now we get to go talk to the cops."

But the cops didn't have much to say either.

"Looks like your daughter has got herself in a lot of trouble," said the very tall, very large and paunchy man behind the desk. "Basically, the procedure is, we call her in, do an interview, maybe find out who her friends are, talk to them. Then it goes to court. The court will make a recommendation, either some form of detention or community hours."

"Well, should we get a lawyer?" Celeste asked.

"That's entirely up to you, Ma'am, if you're willing to spend the money. Basically, this case is pretty straightforward, just a matter of waiting until we get a court date. We'll notify you if there are any changes." He stood up.

Defeated, Louise and Celeste shuffled out of the room and down the street, in silence, to the bakery. They gulped scalding coffee and sugarcake donuts hungrily, silently.

"I hate this town," Louise said at last. "Hey, do you remember the time somone spray painted the town sign so it said Deadview instead of Hill View?"

"People are the same everywhere," said Celeste, automatically. She chewed her donut and stared out the window.

"So what's next?" said Louise. "Doesn't look like you're going to get much help from the school or the cops. So now what do we do?"

Celeste's gaze wandered the room.

"Don't know. I just don't know."

They sat in silence for a while. It was snowing again. It would be slippery getting up Louise's hill if the snowplows and sanding trucks hadn't yet made it out there.

"Well, is that it?" Louise finally demanded. "They put her in a box labelled juvie and that's the end of it?"

"I don't know what else to do. It's all so cut and dried somehow."

"Maybe try another counsellor ..." said Louise vaguely. Then she said. "Oh God, but not Norman."

Celeste shook her head and giggled. "No," she said, "not Norman. Never 'Norman no-man.'"

"Yeah," said Louise. "Pretty hard to sit across a desk with someone you made fun of your whole life and take him seriously."

"Maybe his father bought him that degree."

"Probably. He's sure not smart enough to have bought it on his own."

"Mail order."

"How he got his wife too ... I heard."

"Have to be ... imagine crawling into bed with bug eyes."

"You seen him lately? Got this little paunch, sticks out just like he's pregnant."

"Nothing would surprise me about Normie, the bug boy."

"Not even if he gave birth."

"To a bug."

"Or an elephant!"

They left the restaurant laughing and went outside into the snow laden blue-winter dusk for the long drive home.

Chapter 6

When Louise got home, there was a note on her door. Becky had been and gone. It was just like Becky to show up when Louise wasn't home. Becky had a trick of appearing and disappearing according to some inner schedule that only she understood. Louise crumpled the note and threw it in the stove. Becky was never around when Louise wanted to talk to her. On the other hand, she always seemed to show up when Louise really needed her. Louise looked at the phone. She could try calling, but Becky would probably be out or at her mother's house. She never seemed to spend much time at home.

And there was no point in calling Becky at her mother's place. Someone was always there — lots of someones; usually one of Becky's sisters with a bunch of kids so that it was always too noisy to talk and people kept interrupting or getting on the extension and making stupid jokes.

At least the note meant that Becky was back from Mexico or Thailand or wherever she usually went. Maybe she'd stick around for a while, at least until treeplanting season or dope-planting season, or however she was making a living lately. Even though they'd been friends for years, Becky kept her own secrets. Sometimes Becky told Louise where she was going and what she was doing and sometimes she didn't. Louise didn't like to pry. Becky would tell her someday, if she felt like it. Maybe she thought Louise wouldn't understand, or might even judge her for it.

The house felt colder than usual. Louise shivered while she lit the fire and fed the horses. It had stopped snowing and the stars were clear and crisp in the black sky. She turned the electric blanket on her bed up to high and ran a hot bath before climbing into bed, naked and still damp. God, she thought, electricity is wonderful. She curled up into the middle of the warmth. The edges of the bed were cold despite the blanket. She wanted to read but it was too cold to stick her hands outside of the blanket. The temperature outside must be dropping fast.

The thought of Becky crawled into bed with her and lay on the next pillow, grinning. *What do you want with me?* Louise thought, irritated. *Why do you keep coming by here? I'm not interesting. I never go anywhere, I never do anything. Why do you bother?*

She might ask Becky about drugs in the town. Becky might know something. She knew about a lot of things, but she never said much. She'd call her in the morning. Plus, Louise remembered, she still hadn't solved her money problem. Her stomach twisted. All she'd eaten today were some donuts and toast. Tomorrow, she promised herself; tomorrow, she'd call Stephen and get some money — a loan to tide her over for another month. There'd be pruning work in another few weeks, even if it was still cold.

She turned over in the bed and slept and dreamed and woke to hear the house moaning and muttering to the wind. Branches from the ancient lilacs rubbed and scratched against the walls. Her nose was cold and she buried it under the blankets. "Susan," she said sleepily, out loud, against her will. "Susan … I miss you, I miss you too much." She drifted off and woke again and dozed until dawn.

She woke to the frozen world. Cold tangled itself around her like snarled thorny vines. She dressed fast, her skin flinching from the icy cloth. Going outside for chores was like diving into an icy pool. The snow creaked and scrunched under her feet and the mucus pinched inside her nose as she breathed.

A car whined its way down the road and slammed carelessly into her yard. The motor rattled to a stop. Louise looked out. Becky. Cold and snow never kept her home. In anticipation, Louise had searched the depths of her freezer and found some ancient coffee beans to grind. She should have made some muffins or something but there wasn't much in the house to bake with. When Becky came in, they hugged long and hard.

"Welcome home," Louise said. "Again. How was your trip?"

"Ah," Becky shrugged. "Travelling. You know. Lots of people, lots of airports. Lots of weird places."

No, Louise thought. *I don't know. Why don't you ever tell me?*

They made themselves comfortable, sat with their feet up on the stove drinking cup after cup of coffee. Becky smoked hand rolled cigarettes and Louise had one with her. Then, finally, when they'd got throught the chatter about families and how everyone was doing, Louise told Becky about Celeste and Celia. Becky shook her head impatiently.

"Gawd, you are so naive, Louise," she said. "I've told you before, there's a lot of mean shit goes on in this town; it's an ugly rotten corrupt little bitch of a place but you go on thinking it's your fault you can't get a job, and it's your goddamn fault you don't have any money. Stephen and his cronies are these little white-haired angels who just happen to have a lot more money than they deserve."

Louise shifted uncomfortably. She hated it when Becky started ranting about the town, even though she herself ranted about the town to Celeste. Becky's ranting had an extra edge of bitterness. Louise thought the town was dumb; Becky thought it was vicious.

"C'mon, it's not that bad. Jeezus, I've lived here all my life. I've never seen any particular corruption. What are you talking about?"

"Forget it, forget I said anything."

They sat in silence for a while. Louise bit back a mouthful of angry words. A log in the stove popped and Louise jumped.

"Look, Becky, I just feel I have to do something. The kid could get sent to juvenile detention or some other horror show. You know how she is. She couldn't take something like that; she's just a good kid who made a mistake. I mean, she's a friend. I've known her all her life. We've got some kind of bond. I don't know. She was always a little hellion, but a really good kid just the same. She's just a normal teenager, really."

"No," Becky said, "she's a kid who got caught, that's the only difference between her and a whole lot of other kids."

"You mean there's other kids do this? But who ..."

"Who tells them what to do ... ?" Becky finished slowly. "I'm not real sure. Whoever it is, they're good at hiding their tracks, because no one says anything and dealers got big mouths. It's this tidy little brother/sisterhood, they like to know who's who around them. But I'll tell you something I've never told anyone, and don't you either. Remember a few years back, when I did that brief stint as a youth worker? Got myself fired for telling the head of Social Services he had his head stuck up his ass. Gawd, that was fun. Just wish I'd done it sooner. There's a lot of street kids in that shithole town, more than you'd think for somewhere that small ... kids who've run away, been abused, got into drugs and alcohol … welfare sticks them in cheap ugly places, upstairs over the bars, and there's one ratty apartment building — you know that ugly old yellow place on the way into town? Well, old Noman the bug boy owns it, probably bought it with the money from his Daddy, so of course, that's where all the welfare clients end up. He never does any repairs, just lets people squawk to welfare if they need a light bulb changed.

"Anyway, when I was working, the place was full of kids, and every once in a while they'd all have money and they'd invite me to some godawful party where everyone would end up being sick drunk and they'd all think they'd had a wild time because they couldn't remember anything. They told me they made the money running coke through the border but they wouldn't say who for. I'm pretty sure it was someone local, I distinctly got that impression. I also got the impression they knew if they talked something real bad would happen … in fact, they said a couple of kids had just up and disappeared, whatever that means. But I didn't pay much attention. Kids come and go these days. Who can keep track of them? Who wants to?"

"I never heard of anyone missing a kid."

"Lou, these are kids who, if they go missing, welfare just figures they've drifted on to some other town. Their parents are too drunk or stoned to care, and the cops just lay another report out on the old fax machine and that's the end of it. And maybe the kids were just exaggerating, being dramatic. Who the hell knows."

"Oh," Louise said. She was angry. Most of the time she couldn't figure out why Becky went on being friends with her when she seemed to think Louise was about the stupidest thing that ever walked.

"But you live here. You bitch about the place, you say it's so goddamn rotten, but you always come back," she said.

Becky flung her head back and laughed. "I sure do, don't I? I keep trying to leave and get dragged back here by something. Guess I just love punishment. Guess I'm just a fool for punishment."

Louise said slowly, "But really, Beck, you could do a lot of things. You're smart, you travel, you read, you take courses, you know more about most things than anyone else I know, you know how to figure things out. You understand things. Nobody else I know explains things the way you do."

"You think the world out there wants somebody around who understands things? You think they want somebody smart? Sure I took a million courses. I even got a degree or two … I stopped counting after a while. I took them figuring maybe I could do something about my crazy family and this crazy world, maybe stop people fighting, drinking, killing each other, maybe keep some of my cousins out of jail ... shit. Naw, treeplanting's honest work, even if it is bullshit and half the trees die. Some live. The ones I pray over, eh." Becky grinned.

But Louise was still thinking. "But how'd Celia get to know them — those kids? How did she get involved? Do you think she'd tell me anything if I tried to talk to her?"

"Louise, she's a teenager. They don't talk, man. Think back. You're not that damn old."

"She might talk to me ..." Louise said uncertainly. She was thinking about it. When was the last time she and Celia had really talked, spent time together, had some fun? Maybe part of this was her fault. Maybe she'd been so sunk into the depths of her own life that she'd ignored Celia when she needed someone.

"I guess all I can do is keep asking questions until I find something out," she added finally.

Becky was silent again. Outside the blue day had darkened and softened. It was going to snow again.

"Hey," she said. "You got any food here? Must be damn near lunch. I'm starving."

Louise reddened. "No, I'm right out of groceries," she said. "Have to get into town, I guess."

"You're broke again. Shit, Lou, I figured as much. And you still won't ask Stephen for the money. You'd just as soon sit here and freeze in the dark. Well, dammit, I'll ask him myself. He owes you, Louise, don't you get it? Any judge would award you the money."

Louise stared out the window. Whose life was it anyway? Becky seemed to think it was open season for advice giving.

"I can't," she said.

"Why not? Christ, what's so hot about starving to death? Lots of people have done it. It ain't unique."

Louise rubbed her face with both her hands, took hold of a hank of hair, examined it, curled it around and around.

"Because the whole time I lived with him, I felt like a slut, a kept women. I took his money and lived in his house and ate his damn food and did nothing. I was a lousy parasite, only I didn't realize it. I was grateful he was nice to me. Well, now I hate it. And the only way I can keep from making it worse is to not take any more money, to keep getting by on my own somehow. Even if it isn't so great."

"I just don't get it. I'm sorry. I don't. You lived with that prick. You slept with him, you laughed at his inane jokes and you put up with his inane friends and you got nothing out of it, not even a kid. And now you'd just as soon starve in the dark out of what — pride, stubbornness? Look sweetie, let me explain some facts to you. Men are born with these appendages; these appendages somehow tell them that they get the money and they get the jobs and they get to say what's what, and they even get to keep us around when it amuses them. I figure, if you get a chance to even the score a little, go for it. Besides, what the hell did you ever do that was so wrong? You fell in love. Big fucking deal … So, you ever call her? She ever call you?"

"No," said Louise. "No, I don't call her. What would I say? Look at me. My life is a mess. And it's my fault. That's what she'd say. I could have gone with her. I could have gone back to university. I could have done a lot of things. Instead, I did the easy thing like I've done my whole life. I married Stephen and I knew better. You know? I knew better the whole goddamn time. I think maybe Susan was just a way out … just an aberration in my life. She was here and she was gorgeous and different from anyone I'd ever known and I fell for it. And no, she never calls. And I don't call her. I don't care anymore, Becky. I'm over it."

"Yeah sure, and I'm just a half breed. So, why don't you call her?"

"No," said Louise. "I don't want to."

"Yeah, figures," said Becky. "Gawd, you're stubborn. C'mon, let's go to town and get lunch. I'll treat. I'm starved. And I'll see what I can find out about Celia."

Chapter 7

The axe chimed against the frozen wood. Breathing hurt Louise's nose, even through the scarf she had wrapped around her face. The truck wouldn't run; it was too cold. The cold was hanging in longer than anyone had expected. By now, near the middle of February, it usually started to thaw. Normally, she would have started working again by now. Instead, things had become more and more desperate. Her UIC cheque hadn't come. She'd found twenty dollars in the pocket of an old jacket and that had kept her going for one more week. She'd cooked what was in her freezer and gone to dinner too often at Celeste's. Finally, she'd broken down and phoned Stephen.

He had come out immediately with a load of groceries, in his new car and in his new wool coat with a scarf and a hat and gloves. He'd left a one-hundred dollar bill sitting on the kitchen table beside the groceries. He'd stood there, looking around the dark, cluttered kitchen. She hadn't offered him tea, just waited for him to leave. And he had.

After he had left, she wished desperately that he would come back. Loneliness had smothered her like an old and filthy blanket. She had eaten the food he'd brought; each bite whispered shame and failure at her. She had gone to bed and read until she was exhausted enough to sleep. Even then, she had dozed and awakened again until the light came through the windows.

Now, she was outside smashing the heavy splitting maul into old and knotty blocks of fir. She was almost out of wood. These blocks had been sitting outside the woodshed, ignored, for the past several years, but now they were what she had left.

Her brother was still making noises about having the land logged. "Gotta get to it before break up," he told her. "Make up your damn mind. You're holding everything up." Casually, lightly, he dropped figures into the conversation — astounding figures. In spite of herself, Louise's heart leapt. Possibilities opened — doors, windows, sunshine. Irritated, she shut them again.

Celeste phoned her every day and wept over the phone. Celia had turned into a sullen stranger. Celia wouldn't talk to her parents. Celia snuck phone calls to people her parents didn't know and she wouldn't say who they were. Celia spent her lunch hours at the video arcade, despite being forbidden to go near the place. Celia was failing school.

"Shit," Louise muttered, smashing into yet another complaining log. She reached for the sledgehammer and drove the maul into the wood. The maul stuck fast. She pounded the enormous block of wood on the frozen ground, leaning back and straining her arms, swearing, until the block gave way, ripping and complaining. She leaned on the maul, panting.

Becky, true to her word, had begun asking questions around town. She'd brought Louise what little she had been able to find out. They had sat and tried to figure out what to do next.

"No way have we got a shred of provable information," Becky pointed out. "We need some facts, we need some real information, not just a few stories from a bunch of stoned teenyboppers."

"Even then, what could we do? Is there anyone working with these kids that they trust? Isn't there someone we could talk to. Surely, there's got to be somebody doing something ... someone in charge, doing some counselling, something. Why the hell is it our problem? Doesn't the government pay people to look after stuff like this?"

"Yeah, there's a youth worker. I think it's Sonny, what's his name, Hyrniuk, or something like that."

"Oh, great," said Louise. "He's a nice person, I guess, but talk about useless. I knew him in school. He was a grade behind me. Or two. I think he failed a grade, somewhere. But I'll go talk to him. Better than nothing. Maybe he can do something about Celia. Send her home from the arcade once in a while. Give her a kick in the ass. All Celeste is doing is crying on the phone to me. I told her she had to get tough with the kids, lay down some rules, tighten up, but you know that household. Fuzzy isn't the word. My God, she and Harold dote on those kids, but they can't seem to get organized to save their lives. They make rules and then all Celia has to do is blink her big blue eyes and threaten to cry and they let her do what she wants."

"What about the school? What are they doing?" Becky had asked. "Aren't they supposed to be giving her counselling, giving her something, somehow."

"Yeah, sure, she got one session with a counsellor. Fifteen minutes. Like that. Boom. That was all. They told Celeste that she didn't want to 'disclose' or something, so there was nothing they could do."

Becky was silent for a while. Then she said, "So, it really is up to you."

"What do you mean?"

"Well, no one's in charge. No one's doing anything. You want to help this poor misguided child. So do something. Quit your bitching and lying around being so damn lazy and useless like the rest of us hippie bums."

"Oh, fuck off, Becky. It's not that goddamn simple and you know it. Do what? Gee, I'm such a bright and shining example, maybe I should start doing some counselling. Guess what, kids. Don't do what I did. Or you'll end up just like me!"

"You know what?" Becky said, with no smile at all. "I love you like a sister and all, but you sure are a pain in the ass. You're so into feeling sorry for yourself. It's like you got a broken record going round in your head. Poor little Louise. Dumb little Louise. It's bullshit and you know it. You did the best you could. You married old what's his name figuring you'd have a life and it didn't work out. Well, excuse me, but that happens to damn near everyone. Then you found out you weren't quite the girl you figured you were. Susan was the best damn thing that ever happened to you but when she walked away you went right back to feeling sorry for yourself. You love this place and this land enough to hang onto it and protect it from Mark but you don't take care of it either. And if you're not careful life's going to walk right on by you."

Louise smashed the maul into another block of wood. The maul shattered splinters from the frozen wood, and the block fell apart with little protest. She split several more, then leaned over, hands on the maul, exhausted and panting. It was time to quit. She picked up several pieces of wood and carried them inside. Just as she got in the door, the phone rang. She dropped the wood into the woodbox and grabbed the phone. It was probably Celeste for the third time this morning.

"Hi," she said, but there was only silence on the other end. "Hello, hello, is someone there?" She waited but the phone gave forth only silence. She thought she could hear somebody breathing. After a while she hung up.

Later, as she was making supper, the phone rang again; again, there was only silence on the other end. That night, as she slept curled in her sagging warm bed, the phone rang five more times. By the next morning, she was raggedly tired and furious.

When the phone rang after her morning tea, she grabbed and yelled into it. "Hello! Is anyone fucking there?"

"Louise, it's just me," Celeste's voice was thin and shocked. "Who did you think it was?"

"Oh, Celeste, I'm sorry. It's just this stupid phone. It's been ringing all night, and when I pick it up, no one's there."

"Yeah? These damn rural phone lines. Probably a squirrel's gotten in the shed and chewed up the switches. Don't worry about it. Look, Lou, can you come over? It's Celia. She won't go to school. She's just sitting in her room. She won't talk to me. I asked her if she would talk to you and she kind of nodded. She really likes you, y'know. She still looks up to you. It's kind of chance for a breakthrough, don't you think?"

"But ... Celeste, I mean ... I don't know what to say. I'm no counsellor."

"Yeah, well, fat lot of good they've done for her. See you in ten minutes. Coffee's on."

Louise hung up the phone and leaned against the wall. She and Celia had been so close once — pals. She used to take Celia riding. Almost every week, they'd pack a lunch and go for a long ride. Celia would chatter about school and friends and Louise would listen with half an ear. They'd spot birds and squirrels and make up names for them. Sometimes they'd sing, nonsense rhymes and popular hits with made up words. Louise figured it was the closest she'd ever get to feeling motherly. She'd thought they had a bond, a special bond.

She liked Celeste's other kids but Celia was her pal. The two oldest boys were too much like Harold — they had drifted quickly into a greasy dim world of cars and machines and tools and the back rooms of garages. Celia's older sister, Carol, was hard edged and practical. She lived a somewhat despairing and desperate life in the midst of the gentle chaos that was Harold and Celeste's life. Carol tried hard to bring her mother and father up to the standards she thought they could have; she cleaned her own room, ironed her own clothes, had perfect hair and makeup, and came and went in her family's life almost as a stranger.

Celia's younger sister, Delores, who was only seven, was quiet and timid — her mother's baby girl. A couple of times, Louise had tried to take her riding, but the horses scared her.

But Celia ... Celia had been like Louise, all scabbed knees and goofy daring, her long blond hair in falling-out pigtails, riding her bike too fast, falling out of trees, her room a mess of toys and food and clothes trodden into the rug. Sometimes she had helped Louise with the gardening and pruning.

And suddenly, without Louise really noticing just how it had happened, Celia was a sullen teenager, too busy to go riding. Her pigtails blossomed into a mass of fuzzy dirty blond curls, makeup bloomed iridescently on her face, and her face opened into a blank mask which smiled and said hello but never stopped to talk.

"All right, damn it, I'll try," she muttered. "Fine, just one fine damn mess this is."

Surprisingly, the truck started with only a little resistance. "Must be warming up," she thought.

Celeste looked almost cheerful when Louise arrived. "Starting to warm up," she announced. "About bloody time. I was thinking another ice age must have arrived and they forgot to tell us. She's upstairs in her room sulking, as usual. But I've decided to ignore it. If she wants to sulk and miss school and ruin her own goddamn life, what am I supposed to do? It's not like she's a little kid anymore. She's got to start figuring some stuff out on her own. Right? I can't do everything for her. I've got other kids too, I've got my own life to live. To hell with her."

Louise looked at Celeste, surprised.

"Don't look at me like that," Celeste snapped. "I can't take much more of this. Look, Lou, you know I'd cheerfully lie down in front of a speeding train if I thought it would do her any good. But nothing helps. Nothing I do. I've been doing what you said, trying to be supportive and nice, and hoping she'd remember that I'm her mother and not the Gestapo. So what good does it do? Goddamit, I'm a human being too, aren't I? I have feelings, too. So where does she get off stabbing in the knife every chance she gets. The old serpent's tooth, I think it says something like that in the Bible ... Go talk to her, go. Go! I can't take this anymore!"

Glum but obediently faithful, Louise climbed the stairs and knocked at Celia's closed door.

"Go away," said a muffled voice.

"Cee, it's me, Louise. I want to talk to you." Louise didn't wait for an answer and pushed open the door. The room was a dim wilderness of clothes, paper, books, blankets, dirty dishes and pictures of rock stars torn from magazines.

Louise stepped over the mess to the bed where Celia was lying, her face propped on her hands, staring at the wall. She sat down on the bed but didn't say anything. The silence dragged on.

"The horses miss you," Louise ventured, tentatively. "Maybe you could come over when it gets warmer. We could ride up to that old cabin up the creek — you know, past the falls there. Remember we were going to do that a while back and never got around to it."

"Yeah sure, she won't let me. She won't let me do anything."

"What? Your Mom? She's always let you do what you want, Cee, within reason, but you got to admit, things have been a little tense around here. Your Mom's doing her best."

"Yeah sure, blame it all on me. That's what she does."

Louise couldn't help it. She laughed. "Oh, come on, Cee, quit feeling sorry for yourself … this is a major mess and you can't blame your brothers for this one. This is serious. Maybe you haven't figured it out yet, but this is seriously serious. I mean, packing drugs through the border. Jeezus Murphy. What did you think you were doing?"

She paused, then added carefully, "So, why'd you do it?"

"I didn't do nothing," Celia flashed. "Nothing. I just got blamed for everything, that's all. It wasn't my fault."

"What do you mean, you didn't do anything? Were there other kids there?"

Celia maintained a sullen silence but her face twisted and her eyes filled with tears. One tear rolled a long, lonely mascara track down her cheek. Louise reached out and wiped it away, leaving a black smear.

"Cee," she said gently. "You know I'll do anything I can to help. You know that, don't you?"

After a long pause, Celia whispered, "Yeah. I guess so. But if I tell you something, promise you won't tell anyone else. Okay?"

"Celia, I can't promise that. But I promise I won't say anything to anyone unless I tell you first? So, okay, who else was there?"

Celia sighed deeply. Tears overflowed and spilled down her face. Louise reached over, found some toilet paper in the spilled cacophony of the floor and handed it to Celia.

"I guess," Celia choked out, her voice muffled by the toilet paper, "I guess there was a bunch of us. We'd been hanging out, you know, down by the river."

Louise sighed. She did know: the clearing by the river. It was the heritage drinking place, the place of rituals and teen culture, marked by heaped firepits full of old ashes, broken glass, tire tracks, empty chip packages, pop cans and collapsed Coke bottles.

"Someone was bragging, you know, and flashing money around and, somehow, we ended up in his car, going down across the border to the bar there."

"Jeezus, Celia, you're only thirteen. They let you in the bar?"

"Well, we kinda stayed in the corner. We didn't stay long. Just got some beer and left. And then on the way back, we took the back road, the old river road. So then the guy who was driving stopped the car, and told us we all had to walk through the brush. I was pretty confused."

"You were probably drunk," said Louise.

"Well, not much. I just had one beer. God, it tastes horrible. So anyway, we got out of the car and it was real dark. This guy gave me this package to carry and told me to put it in my pack. So I did. I didn't really think about it. We started walking and I was trying to keep up with the other kids, but they were going so fast. So then we came out on the main river road, and someone yelled, 'Cops,' and everyone ran, only I didn't because I couldn't figure out which way to run. And then they found the drugs and this guy told me that if I told, I'd get really really hurt bad and he'd get into a lot of trouble. Like, you know, serious trouble." She burst into long sobs. Louise rubbed her shoulders.

"So now you're scared to go to school?" Celia nodded, a little scared nod.

"Celia," Louise said gently. "I got to ask. Do you know who gave this guy, the driver, the package? Do you know how he got it?"

"No!" said Celia, so quickly Louise figured she had to be lying.

"Okay," Louise said. "So it's not your fault and you didn't do anything. But now you're in trouble and this other kid is getting off scot free, and your Mom and Dad are crazy with worry. Do you figure that's fair? What's his name?"

"I told you, that's all I know. You said you'd help but you'll just get me into more trouble. So leave me alone," Celia exploded. She buried her head under a pillow. Louise sat beside her for a while longer, rubbing her back, and then gave up and went back downstairs.

"She told me a little bit more," she said hesitantly to Celeste. "But not much. I don't think it was really her fault. Sounds like she just did a dumb thing. Let me ask a few more questions in town, see what I can find out. It won't hurt her to stay home for a few days. Probably do you both good. Maybe if you just hang around together and don't put any pressure on her, things might get easier. If I find out anything more, I'll let you know."

Chapter 8

The next day, Louise figured she'd better talk to Sonny Hyrniuk, the youth counsellor. Only now, it was going to be hard to find the time. The weather had indeed, and suddenly, warmed up. The gravel road outside her driveway was a mess — a layer of wet muck over still-frozen gravel on which the truck slithered drunkenly on its way down or up the hill. The highways were finally bare, although water ran in brown sheets across the pavement and slush still coated the embankments. Snow still lay everywhere across the fields; and the gray cloud ceiling still enclosed the valley in its dark cover. But George, the guy who owned the orchard where she usually worked, had finally phoned that morning.

"Might as well get started. Way behind," George had grunted. "Show up Monday." Not so much as a hello or how are you. But that was George: dour, slow, given to hard work and little speech. When she had started working for him, he had followed her through the orchard, plainly skeptical about her claim that she knew how to prune trees. Once he had seen that she knew what she was doing, he had left her alone to work where and when she wanted. If she worked a lot for the next few weeks, she thought now, she could make some extra money — enough to get ahead a little, buy a new jacket and tires for the truck, hay, food, seeds for the garden, maybe even new linoleum for the kitchen floor. No, that was dreaming. When would she get time to lay linoleum? Next fall, maybe; but there was nothing wrong with a little dreaming. The prospect of having money again left her giddy and euphoric, with a lilting sense of freedom. Spring was coming; she'd be working, she'd have money. She had survived another winter here. There was nothing she couldn't do.

Louise went inside and called the Youth Centre. A bored-sounding kid on the other end said he didn't know where Sonny was and, no, he didn't know when he'd show up. He didn't sound like he much cared. She asked for a home phone number.

"Not allowed," said the voice. She left a message that she had called. Directory assistance informed her that Sonny's number was unlisted. Well, someone must know it.

She went back outside. The yard at this time of year always looked like a dreary wasteland or a battlefield after the bombs had stopped — flattened and oozing mud, water and the black stringy remains of dead plants. Grey branches, dead leaves, horse shit. With her new energy still ringing inside her, she decided to clean it up and keep it clean. She got a rake and scraped at the flower beds. Then she tried to rake the fallen leaves, left over from October, under the apple trees, but they were still frozen to the ground. This year, though, she'd keep to her resolution: get the flower beds dug up and replanted, make new raised beds for the vegetable garden, trade for some plants, look after the old fruit trees — maybe she'd get some new rootstock and graft from the old ones. She could save them. The were heritage apples, part of history, part of her family. Maybe she could even paint the house and build a new wood-shed. As she was wandering the yard, rake in hand, poking at things and making plans, Mark drove in.

He got out of the car and they leaned against it together, both surveying the lumpy mud ruts at their feet.

"Talked to Harold," Mark said, scuffing the ground with his foot, back and forth. Louise watched his boot with its brown faded leather. Why did Mark always wear cowboy boots?

"Figured he could start logging next month or so, soon as it dries up. Figured Harold'd do an okay job. Said he could use Al's cat. Means a bit more money for him. Not much hauling right now."

"Mark," said Louise carefully. "I've been thinking. What if you took my share of the logging money and I bought you out of the land? Do you think that might work?"

"Well, maybe, I guess so, Lou," said Mark. He shrugged. "But I kind of figured you needed the money. You could put some into the house, get yourself a better truck. That old piece of shit's gonna leave you hoofing it one of these days."

"I'm working again," said Louise. "Truck's good for a while yet."

"Well, I dunno," said Mark. "Have to talk to Janet. If you need money now, why don't you go after Steve? He owes you. Man ought to pay up. Maybe I should talk to him."

"Mark, just leave it, okay? So, how much money would we get from the logging?"

"Oh, ten, twelve each, Harold says. Hard to say. We're goin' to cruise it next Saturday. Haven't looked really close. But Jeezus, the price of logs these days. Might as well cash in."

"I should come too."

"Yeah, right, sure, if you want to." He looked doubtful, as if walking through the woods was not quite the right place for her. "Hey, listen Lou — anything you need, you know."

"I'm fine," she said. "Work's starting next week.

"Yeah, right. Well, work is work, eh? Well, gotta go. See ya."

After Mark left, Louise went and got a brush and took some hay to the horses. Carefully, she brushed their thick winter coats. Dust and loose hair floated in the air around her, coated her face and clothes. A stray tendril of sunlight illumined a small patch of the fields below her house. The breeze on her face felt almost warm.

It was true, what Mark had said. She'd known it all along but she hadn't wanted to think about it. All along, she had only to reach out her hand and life would change. She had survived; and now she would even be able to survive well — even if the price was a torn and ugly landscape for awhile. It would grow back. It would look untouched in a few years. This land around her had been logged over once already. Her Dad had said so. The horses stood still, heads drooping in drowsy pleasure at her brushing.

The money would make her different; it would change things, change her, even more than her affair with Susan had made her different. This difference would be an acceptable one, something everyone would understand. With money in her life and in the bank — secure, a bulwark against cold, misfortune, a dead truck, an accident — her steps would loosen, her shoulders straighten. She would be different. Her clothes would be different, her hair would be different. She could afford a haircut.

Clothes and hair. When she had been with Stephen, she had honestly tried — desperately, guiltily, furiously tried. She had gone to the hairdresser, gone shopping. But she hated the hairdresser's. It was like going to the dentist: someone bending over her, breathing on her; and fumes of old permanents, hairspray, deodorant. She would come out at last with her hair primped and curled and sticky — a ridiculous look that only lasted until she could get home and shower.

And clothes — there weren't any clothes she liked. She like blue jeans and plaid shirts and sweat pants and heavy sweaters she could work in. Other clothes felt like costumes. And her hair suited her long and uncut, unshaped and unsprayed.

A new vehicle might be nice. Actually, the truck wasn't in bad shape, once she could get the brakes redone. But the house — she could do some work on the house. Maybe.

What did she really want the money for? To buy the land? But it was hers anyway — hers and Mark's. Would it make a difference if it was all hers? It seemed silly to buy something she already had. It was their bond. She knew he felt the same way, although they'd probably never talk about it. It was theirs. It would always be home, no matter what happened.

What could she do for the house with the money, besides putting yet another coat of paint over the innumerable old ones on the walls? Maybe she could hire a carpenter and do some renovating: new windows, new walls, maybe some insulation. That would be great. She could buy electric heaters so that the house would stay warm; or a new stove. When she started thinking about it, the list grew and grew.

Then there were new bulbs and plants for the garden; new fruit trees; a white rail fence for the pasture. What else? She didn't think she knew yet. She'd have to talk someone about house design. It was exhilarating and confusing, all the possibilities. Maybe that's why she'd never gone after Stephen for money. What she had told Becky about her reluctance to ask Stephen for money was true, but it was more than that. It was always more than that.

She stared at the far blue hills, where yellow streamers of sun made patterns of gold and white against the blue. She needed to know about the possibilities. She felt as if she should be very careful, as if she were walking a terrible foreign field, full of traps, minefields and unknown assailants. If she had money, she would have something to protect; if she had money, she'd have to change. She would have choices to make, things to do in the world, things to do *with* the world — things she didn't care about and had never understood.

She had lived in Stephen's world like an ignorant, awkward child visiting a strange and unknown world. She had managed to learn some of the customs and the language and the voices; she had passed undetected and unseen in that world full of strangers where no one had ever seemed real enough to get to know. She had never given them a chance to know her, never showed herself to them or to him.

"It's not safe," a voice had cried, and she had nodded, thinking: If they knew her, saw her, heard her, would they care? Or would they go on hating or ignoring her, turning a sniggering wall of indifference and superiority towards her? She hadn't known the answer then and she would never know it. Now could she pass there again — on better terms, camouflaged with her own money and new clothes and opportunities?

So here it was — her chance again. She could play the game again, look like them, enter into the world, make choices, go to school, fix up the house, move away. She could enter into the world they had made and make her way there, on their terms and hers as well. Because of money.

She felt it drifting towards her, the soft sibilance of the patterns of this new world shifting around her. Or perhaps it was she who was shifting — trying on new thoughts like bits of jewelry. Money: It would make her safe. It would give her a place in the world, finally.

She finished cleaning the horses and went and put the brushes in their box in the barn. The horses nosed the ground for any last bits of hay, before plodding slowly away from the fence. It felt late, but it was still light out. It really was going to be spring. Soon, she'd be able to work outside in the evenings. "When spring comes," she thought, "when spring comes, things will change."

She turned and went away from the yard, across the road and through the fence to the upper pasture. Small conical fir trees poked through the crusted snow. In eighty years, this field would be forest again.

Her boots crunched through crusted snow that thawed each afternoon and was frozen again by evening. Bits of icy snow fell into the tops of her boots. The field began to seem immense. She thought of turning back, but it would be almost as much effort to go back to the house as to keep going. She stopped for breath and looked at the valley: shades of gold and ochre grass, gray stick trees, burgundy willow fringing the river, the river itself like a sheet of black glass, the smoke from the sawmill far away in the town, drifting up to join the blue-gray haze of clouds. The mountains were walls of white and blue glazed porcelain with the sun shafting through, lighting the valley — her place, her home. Her feet were planted solidly beneath her; her body was breathing, in and out. Her heart opened, expanded like a white flower. She turned and began climbing once more.

She came to the rock bluff at the top of the field. Here the trees were bigger — ponderosa pines, bare ground around their trunks, their flaked bark glimmering ochre red. She kept going, sweating now, to the top of the bluff. It was flat, protected by huge trees and layered in centuries of pine needles — a place she had come to countless times in her life, a place where she had once built a hideout. She had screamed at her brother — chased him screaming like a maniac — when he had told his friends about it. In fact, they had taken it away from her and were using it to practice smoking. But she had got it back. Once, she remembered, she had come here in early spring, like this, and taken off her boots and wet socks and walked on the bare ground — proud in her delight at being able to go barefoot so early in the year. And she had come here at thirteen, humiliated at having a crush on a boy shorter and dumber than herself. She had come here after Susan said goodbye and drove out of Louise's yard and out of her life. Louise had sat, looked at the forty foot fall from the bluff and wondered what to do next, how to keep going; her mouth tasting of ashes, her chest hurting every time she breathed.

She stared at the ground, at the bare place under the trees. Then she sat down to take off her boots and socks, stood up and walked around. She winced. The cold bit savagely at her feet. Hooks from an old pine cone siphoned venom into them. She gave up and replaced her socks and boots. Her socks were wet and almost impossible to get on. Her boots were freezing. Her feet were freezing.

It was almost dark. She looked across the valley. From here she could see the lights of the town. Tomorrow, right after work, she'd go find Sonny. And she'd tell Mark to go ahead with the logging. The trees would grow again. The land would recover, although it would be scarred with cat tracks and skid roads and stumps and cigarette filters and aluminum cans and the harsh adult workmanship of men.

She went back down the hill. It was dark when she reached the house. She stood outside, feeling the loneliness tugging at her like an vicious current as she stood for a long moment looking at the dim yellow light from the windows of her house.

She had stood like this so often before. As a kid, she would ride the whining yellow school bus back and forth to school every day. Every afternoon, she got down out of the bus, her head aching from reading, from the clatter of voices and from the smell of stale lunches, farts and diesel fumes. She would go in the house, silently get a snack or a drink of milk, change her clothes and leave again. She would go up the mountain, past the pine trees and along old trails, the gray dusty noise in her head gradually subsiding. Whatever dog was living on the farm would range through the woods beside her.

When it began to grow dark, she would come home and stand outside in the yard watching the yellow light from the windows, her feet burning and itchy with cold. The wind would curl and mutter through the forest she was leaving. Behind her was cold and black silence and peace. Inside the house was warmth and food and the peculiar silence of the dinner table, where the family exchanged bits of news over the food; there was the refuge of her room and sleep. For a long savoured moment, she would think of turning, of finding her way to a thicket, of curling alone and unseen somewhere in the night; then she would go inside. The moment was only a promise — one she had never kept and had never let go.

She could go to Celeste's. It would be noisy and busy, everyone involved with their own lives. She could go find Becky, but that wasn't the pattern of their relationship. Becky always came and found her. There was no one to call, nowhere to go. There was just herself, the house and the long familiar silence. She went in.

But the phone rang, right after she got in the door. It was Becky.

"Hey," Becky said, "you ever read the paper?"

"Not if I can help it," said Louise. "Nothing in it but the Catholic Women's League news and the hockey scores."

"Yeah, well, last issue, there's an ad. They want people who are interested in going back to school, getting their degree. And then one more year and you get either a teaching or a counselling degree. And you can do it here, you wouldn't have to move away."

"Becky, I don't want to be a teacher or a counsellor. I'd be lousy at those things."

"Yeah? When was the last time you tried?"

"I don't want to try."

"Why not? What have you got to lose? Anyway, I'll meet you at the bakery Monday at five, show you the paper. At least think about it, Lou. You're not getting any younger."

Louise groaned as she hung up. Things were piling up on her.

As she was going to bed, the phone rang again. She picked it up, listened to the silence on the other end. It rang again four times during the night. By morning, groggy and furious, she had decided to call the phone company and damn them to hell if they didn't fix whatever glitch was jolting her awake from a sound sleep, heart pounding in sudden, inexplicable fear.

She had dreamt the phone ringing several times and had awakened to an empty silent house, only to fall asleep again and be jerked awake. It was more than a person should have to stand, she thought.

Chapter 9

"Sonny," Louise said. "Long time no see."

Sonny looked up. It was early evening and he was standing outside the 7-11 store, talking to a group of boys who were leaning against the hoods of cars. The cars were parked in a rough circle, nose to nose, taking up most of the parking lot and barely leaving room for other cars to squeeze through so that the people in them could buy gas and Cheezies and Coke.

The cars looked sleek, polished. They squatted, like crouching animals, and shone silver-blue, purple or black in the violent glow from the streetlight. Their fat tires rested on the oil-stained pavement. The boys leaning against them looked young and frail — too young to be driving these snarling muscular cars. All the stereos in the cars were playing and each one had a different beat. Bass notes pulsed in the reeking air, mixing with gasoline and car exhaust — blue misty fumes.

The boys ignored Louise when she called out to Sonny; they looked through her like she was made of air. Sonny looked up and came towards her. He said something to the boys, but they ignored him as well. His shoulders drooped. His hair was thin and greasy, slicked back over his head, and he hadn't changed much since school. He and Louise had been in the same classroom for a few years, when there were combined classes. There had been one room and one teacher — Mr. Foster, yelling and throwing chalk. She remembered Sonny's white sad face during spelling bees, an activity Louise had excelled at. She had liked Mr. Foster, even though he threw chalk, because he let her read in class and thought she was brilliant at spelling and art. Which she had been.

What a horrible job, Louise thought, hanging out with these little monsters. Bet they could care less what ideas Sonny comes up with for youth activities.

Sonny came up to her. He was shorter than her, with a round pudgy face and thick glasses. He had always looked like that, she thought, only now he was bigger and older. She remembered also knowing him as one of a number of loud and fairly stupid boys, given to tormenting the girls on the playground when they weren't playing incessant, obsessive games of soccer.

"Sonny, how's it going?" she said, uneasily. "Can I, uh, buy you a coffee? I need to ask you about something."

"Sure," he said, but he looked unhappy about it. They walked across the street to the Chinese restaurant. When they were settled in a booth, Louise said, "Sonny, I want to talk to you about Celia. You know, Celeste and Harold's kid."

"Yeah, I know her. She hangs around the Centre. I figured that's what it was. What's the problem?"

"Look, Sonny, there's things here I don't quite understand. Celeste and I talked to the police and the school, and we didn't get anywhere. I managed to talk to Celia. Finally. She told me some of what happened. Sounds like it wasn't her fault."

"What do you mean?" said Sonny. "She got caught red-handed, didn't she? So now she's trying to weasel out of it. So what's that got to do with me? Who does she say did it?"

Louise sat back and looked at him. His face was sullen, closed. "She was set up," Louise said. "Someone is behind this, someone must be setting it up. Maybe she isn't the only one. Maybe some other kids are involved too. I thought you might know something that would help."

Louise hesitated. Sonny was drumming his fingers on the table in an uneven beat that rattled the thick coffee cups and the empty sugar container. He twisted his mouth to one side.

"These are just ordinary kids — nice kids from nice homes. They might get out of line once in a while, get caught drinking a few beer when they shouldn't, drag racing on the river road, you know … same stuff we used to do, but on the whole, they're no worse than any other kids." He stared out the window while he talked, then twisted around to look at the parking lot — anywhere but at her.

"You're the youth worker, right? You work with these kids, hang around with them. I don't really know what you do, but you're around them a lot. You listen. You know how they think, how they talk, right? You know what's ..."

"I know a few things," Sonny interrupted her. "I know what they tell me, sure, but that's not really my job. I keep the youth centre going, I organize activities. I keep the place clean and functioning. I'm not a babysitter or a handholder or a fink. I'm the recreational activities coordinator."

"But surely you have some idea who is using drugs and who isn't, or who's got money and who doesn't. You'd know, for example, if someone was dealing, or bringing drugs through the border."

"I'm not a cop," he said sullenly. "That's not my job. I'm a social worker. You may not know, but I got my degree from a university in the States. I'm here to do counselling, listening, organizing and, if I need to, I can talk to the proper authorities."

Louise's heart raged at the open sneer in his voice. "So you're saying you don't know anything. Celia got caught. Boom, that's the end of it."

"It's a police matter," said Sonny. "I don't quite understand just why or how you have any concerns with it. I'm sure if there's anything more to find out, they'll take care of it. And now, if you don't mind, I'm supposed to be working. I've got things to do."

After he left, Louise sat and stared into her coffee, as if it held some answers. She wondered if he had learned that particular tone of voice at Social Work school, if they had a class in Proper Speech to Use with Stupid People. He had also been very uneasy. "This is weird," she muttered out loud. "This is really, really weird."

She went back across the street to the 7-11. The cars were still parked, hood to hood, and the boys were still leaning against them. All of them were smoking. A group of girls in denim jackets and jeans huddled together near the boys. Both groups were pretending to ignore each other. There was no sign of Sonny.

She went inside. The place was full of people and there was a lineup at the counter. What was the attraction? She stared at the magazines for a while, bought a ginger ale and some chips and went home.

Chapter 10

The next day was Monday. Louise got up at six, lit the fire, fed the horses and went to work. Settling into familiar work was a relief. The trees were crowded with thin water shoots, suckers sprouting straight up from the branches like invasive upstarts. "Damn trees are suicidal," she thought, in her father's voice. "Trying to strangle themselves."

All day, she lifted and set ladders, climbed up, cut and shaped branches in a trance, moving like a sloth around the tree in a graceful ancient dance. As she worked her way steadily down the row of trees, thoughts of Celia, Sonny, the town, Celeste, drugs, Mark and logging blew through her head like dust devils whirling over a dry field. At least she would see Becky after work, she thought — that would help. She needed to talk to Becky about Sonny, and Mark; she needed to ask her if logging the land was the right thing to do. She just needed someone. She felt suspended in her life, in the middle of many decisions, all needing attention.

After work she drove to the bakery, got her tea and donuts and sat down happy from a day of good work done. Tree dirt was in her hair, green and brown stains were on her hands, she had a good, earned stiffness in her legs and she was waiting for Becky to celebrate spring and work and surviving.

But Becky had her own problems.

"Oh, my crazy family," she groaned, holding her head in her hands. "Just when I think they're doing okay, it all falls apart again."

Louise had never understood Becky's relationship with her family although she knew them well. For three years, they had lived on the old homestead next to her family's place, until, restless as birds, they had moved on again. Now they had another large farm, twenty miles from town and ten miles from her house, where they seemed, finally, to have settled. Most of Becky's brothers and sisters lived close by, scattered over the valley. About once a week or more they all got together to eat and talk at the top of their lungs, everyone at once. Louise had been friends with them from the day they moved in next door. She still went to visit and was invited for birthdays, occasions, celebrations and the odd mournful, loud, drunken wake whenever the family lost one of its innumerable cats, dogs, horses or other pets.

"Lou, you gotta come to dinner. My sister's back home again; it turns out her old man has been a total jerk all along and she never bothered to tell us. I guess he slapped her around a few times and she was scared. Jeezus, you think she'd know better. Anyway. You got to come over. My mother's having a fit. My father won't talk to anyone. My brothers are swearing they're going to go cut his balls off. My sister won't stop crying or listen to anyone. If you come, they'll stop fighting. They might even listen to you. They like you, better than they like me, most of the time."

Becky stared moodily around the room. "Men," she said. "Goddam perverted bastards. I wish to God I didn't enjoy sleeping with them. You're lucky. At least, you have an alternative. I don't know why you don't take more advantage of it. You ought to give her a call."

"Becky, what's this school thing you were talking about?" Anything, Louise thought, to change the subject.

"Oh, yeah." Becky pulled a torn piece of newsprint from her pocket. "Yeah, it looks okay. It's some American school, advertising for students. You do most of the work here, and then you go south for three weekends a year. Sounds great. You can make up your program, choose a degree. Why not? Look: counselling psych, women's studies, ecological studies, whatever the hell that is, and then a few more courses and you have a teaching degree if you want one."

"What the hell good is a degree going to do for me in this rat hole, except cost me a lot of money?" Louise snapped. "There's no work here, degree or no degree, you know that, except for idiots like Sonny Hyrniuk. Besides, how am I supposed to pay for school. I make it from month to month, barely."

She decided abruptly that there no point at all in mentioning to Becky that she and Mark might log the farm. "Anyway, I talked to Sonny," she ventured.

"Oh yeah ... how did that go?"

"Oh, he said he was a coordinator, not a babysitter. Told me that he had a degree, like it was some kind of very big deal. Maybe he knows something. Maybe he just still resents me for beating him up in third grade. Who knows? I can't figure this situation out. It doesn't make any sense. Celia says she didn't do it. Of course she would say that. Except she sounds like she means it. She sounds scared. She says if she talks any more, she'll just get into trouble."

Becky grabbed her hand across the table. "Lou, be careful," she said, very quietly. "This maybe is not a good situation. Maybe Celia is talking good sense."

"Becky, for pete's sake. We've both lived here our whole damn lives, we know this town. It's just an ordinary, boring, jerky kind of place. There's no big criminals, just a bunch of smalltime ordinary people with nothing better to do than gossip about each other and make stuff up."

Becky looked around the room and her face twisted. "Sure, an ordinary town. Ordinary people. Salt of the earth. Buying, eating, fucking, making money. Bitch a little, get drunk, beat the little wife and then you die. Great life. Sorry, I gotta go. Don't forget. Dinner on Sunday."

Louise could see herself reflected in the glass window of the bakery. It was already dark out. The woman in the glass stared back — mysterious, and even, somehow, dimly beautiful. "Susan." Silently, Louise shaped the name. She rolled the vowels around her tongue. Susan's breasts under her hands. Susan's belly rising and falling. Laughter. Susan laughing.

Louise had spent hours wondering about Susan: What could they do? What could she do? She had tried to picture Susan in her house, in her bed, in her life. She imagined introducing her to friends, to Celeste, to Harold. But fear had grabbed her and split her to the root, had driven a knife wedge into her most private heart. She could do what she wanted as long as she was alone; she could live how she wanted. But she couldn't do that with Susan, not here, not with these people, not in the glass kettle, where she and everyone else bubbled around in a stew of their own making. She knew how it went. She'd done it so often — she and Celeste: Dissecting somone, laughing at them, their contempt mixed with relief that the two of them were there, talking, being friends, making a wall against the world. With Susan, she would be at *their* mercy. It would be like walking down the street naked. It was better this way: better alone, better hidden — even if the price she paid was getting into her truck every night and driving home alone and listening to silence drip from the rafters, the slow rain of years.

In her silent house that night, Louise picked up yet another block of wood and began carving. There was a horse in the wood. She could almost see it. By the time she went to bed, she had the outline chipped and hacked out. Too tired to work any more, but unable to sleep, she lay still under her heap of covers. Her eyes itched and burned, but no matter what she did they obstinately stayed open and watched the night pass.

The next day, at work, the talk at lunch turned to drugs and drug dealing. The men who worked in the orchard were a mixed bunch; she never got to know any of them very well. They came and went. Some worked long enough to get a paycheque. Some stayed for a whole season, long enough to get a UIC claim and move on. She was the only woman on George's crew, and the only worker who came back every year. Sometimes she saw one or two of the other workers in town or in another orchard.

There was a shed where George provided a wood stove and a table. Louise brought her lunch and a thermos and usually she ate by herself somewhere in the orchard, leaning against a tree; today, she deliberately joined in the conversation.

"Any of you ever hear of kids being used to carry drugs through the border?" she asked.

"Hey, man, anybody stupid enough will do," muttered the man next to her.

"Man, I was carrying one time. Walked through some back road for five hours. Whoa, paranoid or what. Must be easier ways to make money."

"Shit, there's tons of drugs come into this here town. Tons, man, just ask at the Elkhorn, man. Get you anything you want ..."

"Hey, I heard they've got cameras now, all along the border. Some guy was telling me they can see you from outer space. Can't get away with nothing, no more. Man, they watch you all the time."

The guy sitting next to Louise rolled a cigarette with a shaky hand and said, shaking his head, "I heard some kids got busted the other day. Said they was loaded with coke. Man, this younger generation. Where do they get off like that? I seen some kids the other day, blue hair, orange hair, green hair. I just don't get it. Like they was Martians or something."

"What else did you hear about these kids?" Louise asked. "One of them's a friend of mine. I'm trying to find out what really happened. I think she got stuck with some else's bad luck. It wasn't her that was supposed to be carrying the drugs. Someone must have set these kids up. Someone must know something."

"I heard there's Mafia in this town," someone else said.

"Naw, ain't Mafia, just some of the local business guys making a few extra bucks. You're this close to a border crossing with a lot of back roads, what the hell. Bound to happen. Best thing is not to ask too many questions in the wrong places."

"Hey, yeah, and then there's them drug growers. Them guys make a fortune, tax free. Lazy shits ... and us here, busting our asses for peanuts. Goddamn George always shorting our checks." The man's voice was aggrieved. Louise looked at him. A thin, bitter, resentful face, crusted with beard growth, red eyes.

"He's never shorted my check," she said.

"Yeah?" said the man. "Well, the stupid old fart better not try it on me any more or I'm gonna get my own back. He'd just better watch it, the old coot."

There was silence in the shed. Louise muttered something and left, went back to the cleanliness of the trees and her silent work among them.

Chapter 11

Louise was coming home from Becky's parents' house when she saw the foggy red glow on the horizon. It was behind a hill and she didn't pay much attention to it except to note the unusual colour. Maybe it was the moon, car headlights, someone's tractor lights, a meteorite, some fool of a farmer getting in some really early spring plowing late at night. Her head was full of noise. She was still recovering from the evening, her head buzzing from the combined effects of being in several conversations at once, beer and the impact of too many people, who knew each other too well, yelling, laughing, bitching and occasionally snarling at each other — at which point, the conversation would come to an uneasy pause and then resume as loudly as ever.

A visit to Becky's parents' house was an event she looked forward to and then was greatly relieved to get away from. For once, she was glad to be heading back to her own quiet house. Even her familiar loneliness was welcome, sitting in the corner of the truck seat like a faithful dog, with maybe a bitter green tinge because she had spent the whole evening with someone else's family. Even when Becky's family fought, and they always did, they stuck together.

She had arrived early enough to help with the dinner, if any help was needed. Becky had seven brothers and sisters and Louise was amazed to notice that almost all of their cars were in the yard. She drove in past the several happy dogs having a visit of their own, a pile of sawmill trimmings waiting to be cut and several ancient, rusting trucks in differents stages of dismemberment. They were parked randomly here and there in the tall grass, with bushes and even small trees growing up through their frames.

The house was rich with the smell of roasting meat, cigarette smoke
and beer; and it was loud with several discussions being carried on at
top volume, over the noise from the television and the rock music in
the basement where the kids had been sent. A turkey crackled and spat
juice in the oven. Becky's dark, calm mother was peeling potatoes in the
midst of it all, perched on a stool at the kitchen table. Becky's dad was
Irish — a tall giant of a man with legs like tree trunks and shoulders like
slabs of knotted wood. He slouched in his chair in front of the
television. His sons slouched in chairs beside him. They all looked like
him — dark, broad shouldered slabs of men, eyes fixed on the television, each with a beer in one hand and a cigarette in the other.

Like his sons, Becky's father was a quiet man with a tendency to get
louder and louder as he drank, which he didn't do often — only when
there was a suitable excuse for it. Occasionally, when drunk, he would
take offence. One Christmas dinner Louise had attended, he had
simply, for some reason she hadn't caught, turned over the table loaded
with food and stomped away outside. The dinner was rescued, more
food was cooked and one of the youngest children was sent to fetch
Grandad. He came in looking chastened and the dinner proceeded as
loudly as ever.

Becky's mother was native Indian, or part native, but, to Louise's
knowledge, no one ever said anything about where she was from or
how she had come to meet Becky's Dad. Becky never mentioned her
mother's side of the family, although her father's relatives were numer-
ous and regular visitors. Sometimes Becky called herself a halfbreed, or
a Cree or an Apache. But she never really talked about it. It was an area
that Louise was always curious about but never mentioned. When the
subject of native people, or Aboriginal rights or tragedies came up,
which it rarely did, they skirted around it; but Louise still wondered.

The whole family gathered at Becky's parent's house for regular
Sunday dinners and occasional consultations during crises or events
like births and deaths and accidents. The parents lived now in an old
log house, set on a cottonwood-studded flat by the river. They had a log
barn, a corral and several cows and horses that grazed among old car
bodies and tractor parts. Right now, the house was too small for the
number of people crowded into it, but no one paid any attention to that.
There were always card tables and extra chairs carted in from somewhere. Athough only Becky's mother and father usually lived in the
house, there were always kids or relatives coming and going. Right
now, Becky's sister Serena was living there with her three kids. Becky,

when she was home, lived in a small travel trailer in the back of the place, close to the river.

Louise insinuated herself into the crowd, accepted a beer from someone and tried to figure out who was there and who wasn't. Stories swirled around her like currents and eddies in a river. The women were all in the kitchen cooking, drinking beer and snacking as they cooked. A row of desserts lined one of the counters.

The men hunched on the sofa and chairs in the living room, uneasy on the soft furniture, which was only ever used during dinners like this. The rest of the time, everyone gathered in the kitchen. The children drifted from group to group, listening, perching on convenient knees or draping themselves over shoulders, being absentmindedly teased or tickled until they tired of it and ran away to some other distraction.

"Heard you're back working for George again," someone said to Louise. "That George ... the old tightwad." (This to the whole kitchen.) "Remember when Danny was working for him? He was just a teenager and George never did pay him what he owed him. Said he wasn't worth it. Poor kid. His first job too. One night, George's tool shed went up in smoke. They never figured out who did it ... Danny always said it wasn't him, but what the hell. Turned out the stupid bastard was too cheap to buy insurance ... served him right ..."

Louise had heard this story before, with details that varied depending on who was telling it. It provoked a round of stories about abusive, cheap, sadistic bosses in various jobs people had held and the techniques used to outwit them, until the tone changed and the conversation turned abruptly, with no contradiction at all, to the difficulty that Jimmy and Danny, who were logging contractors, were having finding anyone to work for them, and how lazy most people were — like those useless bastards who worked for a few weeks and then went on unemployment. Becky simply smiled over the salad greens she was chopping and lifted her eyebrows at Louise. If it wasn't for UIC, Becky had pointed out to her a few times, the whole valley, along with her family, would have starved to death years ago.

When card tables had been set in the living room for the kids and all the children had been rounded up and it had been settled which child was sitting where and next to whom; and when the men had been coaxed and bullied to the table, and the dinner table had been loaded with food, there was a moment of silence while everyone contemplated the rich simmering mountains before them: white potatoes, sweet potatoes, squash, green beans and corn, cauliflower and broccoli with cheese sauce, salad, pickles and olives, biscuits and rolls and platters of sliced turkey and ham. Then they ate. The talk died to a murmur while they loaded their plates and made it through the first helping; by the time the bowls and platters were going around a second time, the talk had risen to a roar again. Now, because of the forced proximity of the men and women of the family, the voices became louder and more competitive and the stories took on a raunchy edge — became crude, gross and boastful.

Louise wondered if they would ever get to the part Becky had mentioned — having some sort of family conference about Serena. She looked around the table. She was always somewhat surprised that these people she had known as children — been a child with herself — were now grown up, capable, strong and often quite responsible people. Their lives had all happened without any of them planning anything. Jimmy and Dan between them owned hundreds of thousands of dollars worth of logging equipment. Judy and Joelle had both been married twice, had children and had done various things for money — sold cosmetics and worked as secretaries, bookkeepers and waitresses. Now they had opened a pet grooming shop together. Serena was the one they protected and worried about the most. She had never been able to hang on to a job, and now it appeared that she couldn't hang on to a man either. Becky's youngest sister, Noreen, was married and had somehow got herself off to college. The family all complained loudly about the fact that she never came home and that her husband didn't know anything about farming or logging. He was an accountant, or some such thing. When Noreen and her husband did come for a visit, the men didn't know what to say and tried to talk about machines, logging or trucks, while the accountant struggled manfully to understand. Becky's oldest brother was a drunk and seldom came home. Only Becky had remained single, which was a source of endless teasing and speculation within the family.

Becky was dark, like her mother Marie. Marie was the only person that the whole family would unequivocally listen to, on the very few occasions when she raised her voice or stated her opinion. Everyone in the family went to her with their problems. When there was too large a disagreement, both people told Marie their side and, somehow, the dispute went away. Mostly Marie cooked and cleaned and cooed over her grandchildren and bought them whatever they wanted that she could afford. When something needed settling, she phoned everyone and invited them to dinner. Somehow, between the mountains of food and the varied conversations, things got sorted out.

When dinner was finally over, the men went back in front of the TV, the kids went downstairs and the women did the dishes and discussed Serena's husband. He had another woman, they said, and he had bashed Serena around; he was a rotten skunk. Jim and Dan should talk to him, should give him what he had coming, should bash him around — let him find out what it felt like. Serena should have known better, should never have married someone with such a lousy reputation. She had always had bad taste in men — look at the creeps she went out with in high school. She never seemed to learn.

Serena sat at the counter, said nothing, drank cup after cup of coffee. Finally she left. When she was gone, the talk became more sympathetic. The kids were upset. They missed their Dad, but the stupid bastard was going to try and go for custody. He obviously didn't give a shit about Serena. He was just trying to get back at her.

"He's a control freak," said Joelle, who went to Al-Anon and read self-help books she bought at the drugstore. "He needs help."

"Jesus Christ, that's what you say about everyone," said Judy.

"She needs to go talk to Legal Services," said Becky. "She needs counselling, someone to talk to. She's the one who needs help."

Marie shut the door firmly on the dishwasher.

"If they try to take the kids, we'll just hide them," she said firmly.

"Mom, we can't do that," said Becky. "They have laws against that kind of shit."

"Don't you want to help your sister?" Marie said gently.

"Of course, I'd do anything ..."

"Well. Then we'll do what we have to. They're our kids. This family sticks together. Don't you go badmouthing your sister when she's having such a bad time."

"I'm not ..."

"Them lawyers don't know nothing about kids," said Marie firmly. "Kids need their mother."

Becky rolled her eyes.

"I gotta go," Louise said. "But thanks for having me. It was great."

Outside, it was cold and clear but not freezing. She could smell the earth, the river, the mouldy ripeness of last year's leaves. She was glad to leave. She had often thought, wistfully, that it must be some solace to belong to something as obvious as Becky's family. Tonight, she had found herself envying the kids their carefree exuberance, their knowledge that, whatever lap or shoulder they were crawling upon, they were welcomed and accepted. They had a place. They were unlike her; she was outside, on the edge of everything.

The glow in the sky got stronger as she turned down the river road towards home. Slowly, the realization crawled into her consciousness that it must be a fire. She drove faster. She came around the corner, started up the hill and saw her house burning.

There were cars parked on the road; there were bodies and faces that looked at her as she slammed her truck to a halt and leapt, running, from the cab.

In the clear night, the fire burned straight up, its centre twisting and roiling with ferocious energy. The heat scorched her face from a hundred feet away. Even as she ran towards her burning house she knew there was nothing to be done. An arm like a wall reached out and stopped her. Harold.

The fire burned like a live thing, growling and wrenching and exploding as it devoured her house, her furniture, her bed, her clothes, her plastic radio, her photographs, her mother's knickknacks, the layers of linoleum and paint and wallpaper, her plants, the just-started carving of the horse. Louise stared, trying and failing to believe it.

Her eyes watered from the smoke, were seared by the heat. Pictures unreeled drunkenly before her eyes, flashing like strobe light: the sunlight through the vines on the front porch; the woodstove in the kitchen; her mother turning around from the stove, smiling, holding out a spoon full of new apricot jam; the exact burgundy of the chair by the stove in the living room, yellowish-gray stuffing seeping from the arms like pus from wounds; her navy-blue bedcover; her blue painted bedroom; an ancient yellow curling picture of her grandmother, found and saved and put up on the wall; her father's boots, which she had never bothered to throw away, still hanging from a nail in the stairwell.

An arm went around her shoulders. Celeste. "We tried," she said. "There wasn't much we could do. By the time we got here, it was already pretty advanced. The Hewletts up the road saw   and called us, but we got here too late. Oh, Louise, I'm so, so sorry."

"Old house," rumbled Harold from the other side. "Went up like a bomb. Your Dad always said it was a fire trap."

"But how? ... How the hell did it start?" she said, desperately. Her voice sounded tinny and far away. "I didn't leave a fire on because it's so warm. There wasn't any fire. How did it start?"

"Could have been anything …" said Harold. "Clothes dryer, extension cord, coffee pot."

"I don't have any of those," Louise's voice rose.

"Mice then; maybe chewed the wires. Who knows? Goddam christly shame. Beautiful old place." Harold's voice cracked. He shrugged and moved away to stand with the men, who were discussing whether or not they should fell the trees nearest the house to keep the fire from spreading.

Someone went and pulled a chain saw from a truck, and someone else restrained him. There were hoses lying on the ground where people had tried to fight the fire, but no one was holding them now, except for two people who were wetting down the woodshed and the old barn with its few dusty bales of hay left inside. There was a forestry pump as well. People had tried. A few people she didn't know were standing in clumps, staring. The horses were standing nervously, far away on the other side of the fence, staring at the fire and the commotion in their normally peaceful lives.

People Louise knew came up to her and said awkward things. They shuffled and shifted their feet in front of her and wandered away. Some people even looked like they'd been crying. Other people began to leave.

"Maybe you'd better c'mon home with me, Lou," said Celeste. "We'll come over first thing in morning, see what we can do. The men will do anything here that needs doing." She tugged at Louise's arm.

Louise nodded but went on standing still. Celeste stood beside her and tugged at her arm a few more times but Louise paid no attention. Finally, she gave up and sent Harold back home to stay with the kids. Shortly after he left, Becky arrived. She came without speaking, took Louise's hand and stood there. The three of them stood watching, the fronts of their bodies scorching hot and their backs freezing cold. A few times they turned around to warm their cold backs at the fire. Someone brought coffee and sandwiches, and someone else brought blankets and laid them over their shoulders. People kept coming and going. There was a continuous flow of traffic in and out of the yard. Headlights flickered off the trees, the barn, the smoke. People stood around and drank the coffee and ate the sandwiches. Louise couldn't make sense of any of it.

She kept thinking, "This is the worse thing that has happened to me."

Then she thought, "How will I survive this?"

She thought desperately, as if seeking some odd comfort, about the other painful, horrible times in her life: when her mother, and then her father, had died; when Susan had left; when she had left Stephen. She tried to remember how they had felt but she couldn't. The fire took all the room in her thoughts and left her full and numb and unable to move. She couldn't take her eyes off it.

The fire took all night to eat the whole house down to glowing coals. Things inside crashed and banged and popped. Windows crashed. Rafters fell, writhing, in the coals. Walls fell in with spectacular showers of sparks. The cold clear sky was laced with sparks among the stars.

Celeste, Louise and Becky stood and stood without speaking until there were only glowing embers left of the house — embers which winked and shifted and muttered in the very faint dawn light, like a nest of strange, red, glowing worms.

Chapter 12

"But how the hell did it start?" Louise asked the wide-bellied fire marshall who was poking reluctantly at the ashes with the toe of his black polished boot.

"Dunno," he said. "Could have been anything. Wires … these old houses, you just never know."

"The wiring was fine. My Dad redid it just before he died."

"No insurance?" the marshall said, checking the chart on the clipboard in his gloved hand. "No injuries? Approximate amount of damage?"

" I don't know," Louise muttered. "Everything I own."

"Well, that's all I can do for now. You'll get a copy of the report," he said, briskly putting things away — pen in the pocket, clipboard under the arm.

Louise said, blurting it out, biting her lips as she said it, "Could you tell if someone set it?"

For the first time since they had met at the still-smouldering pile of ashes, metal, burnt wires and scrap that had been her home, the man actually looked at her.

"You got any reason to think it might have been?" he said. His eyes were glinting. His jacket buckles shone in the sun. He was much taller than she, and he had to look down to see her.

She hesitated. He saw the hesitation and waited. Louise said nothing. Finally he said, frowning and impatient, "Look, I don't have time for this. I got to get back to the station. If you think of something you want to tell me, give me a call." He handed her a card, walked up the hill, got into his brand-new, white, official fire marshall's car and drove away. She watched the dust from his car make a trail down the hill.

Then she went and examined the remains of the house. Twisted, barely recognizable shards and coils of metal reared up from piles of charcoal and scorched wood. The stove still stood attached to the remains of the partly crumbled brick chimney. She bent and tried to open the door. It was too warped.

"Burnt remains," she said out loud. "Toast. Fricasseed. Barbecued." She knew she was feeling crazy and she tried to stop herself. She went around and around the ashes, circling them like a thief trying to enter a locked room. "What are you going to do what are you going to do what are you going to do," she keened, circling and circling, while a wind came and danced among the ashes with her and sent the reek of burning back into her face.

She sat down, although she didn't want to. What she wanted to do was walk down the road, walk and walk until she found her home, her chair, her stove, her radio, her kettle, her faded rug and dusty walls; she wanted to walk and walk until she found a place to be quiet, where no one would look at her ever again, where they might miss her and ask where she had gone although she would have escaped forever any obligation to figure out what to do and how to cope and why no one ever looked at her anymore and and why any and all of her life had happened to her.

But she didn't. She sat and then she trudged around the sad, dead pile of ashes that was still smoking at one corner. She poked it with her own boot one more time and then got in the truck and drove to Celeste's house. She parked and came inside and had coffee and talked to Celeste as if everything were normal in the world. When she couldn't stand it any longer, she went and lay on the couch and watched TV and listened to life going on around her until she couldn't stand that anymore either, and then she went outside and got in her truck and sat there, wondering what to do.

Finally, she started the truck and drove to Stephen's office. She drove badly on the way in. She knew she wasn't thinking clearly and wasn't reacting clearly — but so what? She parked outside Stephen's office and walked in. His door was open so she walked past Bimbette, who didn't try to stop her, and into his office.

"Okay, Stephen," she said, "You win. You're right. I need the money. I'll take it. Give me something to sign or something. I don't care."

He peered over his glasses at her, crinkled his brow, pursed his lips, the very picture of an innocently astonished man. "Money ... I'm sorry, you've sort of lost me here. You've lost some money? Did you have it stored in the house?"

"Stephen, I need money. I don't have a house or a place to live. I need to do something with my life. I can't go on like this. Look at me. I have nothing, I am nothing ..."

Her voice choked. Her throat closed off. She coughed the words back into her throat. She couldn't breathe. She coughed and coughed. Stephen came around the desk and offered her a glass of water.

Gently, he ushered her to a chair, lowered her into it and said, very patiently and calmly, "Now I understand that you're upset, but I'm not sure what we're talking about here. You think I owe you some money?"

"You said ..." Her voice wouldn't come out right. It bent and twisted like a willow branch in the wind. "You said, when you sold our house, that part of the money should be mine. You offered me money, remember?"

"Yes, and you turned me down flat, as I recall, and said, let me be accurate here, that you would be just fine without any help from me. And, just to be totally accurate, I never offered you money from the house. I offered to support you until you got on your feet. And you were quite right. You seem to have managed fine without help from me."

"Stephen, I need help. I don't have anywhere to live anymore. I don't have a house. I don't have a home."

"Yes, well, that is terrible. I know how you feel. You must have left something plugged in, the iron or something. You always were a tad forgetful." His voice was very gentle.

"Stephen," she said. She forgot about her own voice and it came out flat and loud. "Stephen, just give me that goddamn money or I'll sue."

A ghost of a smile hovered around his mouth.

"Well, you could sue, I suppose; you might even get some money, eventually. It would be expensive for both of us, and take a long time. But, since you're obviously going through a bad time, I'll make the same offer I made before; I'll help out temporarily, until you figure out what you're going to do. My advice would be to sell. The place is actually more saleable with that house gone. It was an eyesore. It would have cost a fortune to fix it up. Been let go too long."

"How much?" she snapped.

"What?"

"How much? What are you offering me?"

"Well, I was thinking three or four hundred a month ... let's say, for a year or two at the most. It's all I can afford right now. That on top of you working should make it possible for you to manage, maybe rent a place in town until you and Mark sell."

"We're not selling the farm," she said very quickly and very loudly, absolutely astonished at the words coming out of her mouth. "And I don't want support. I don't want a piddling bit of money every month. I want a whole lump of money. I want enough to build a new house. I want a place of my own. And then I'm going to school. I'm not living in town, in some jerky little rental place, where you and everybody else can look down at me and laugh. I'm not. I couldn't stand it. You know that. You can give me that money now willingly or I'm going to see a lawyer, a real lawyer who'll make you look like chickenfeed … You're so damn smug … you're cruel. Jeezus, I'm not asking for favours here, I'm asking for what's mine. You said it was mine. You said I could have it for the asking. I need it now! You bastard!"

Her voice was still doing things without her control, rising to a high-pitched roar that didn't even sound like her. Any second now she was going to burst, going to sob and wail and howl out loud and make a fool of herself. She choked and coughed, stood up and blundered her way out of his office onto the sidewalk. She stumbled to the truck, climbed in and leaned shakily on the steering wheel.

Someone rapped on the window. It was Becky. Louise fell out of the truck and into Becky's arms and onto her shoulder. After a while, she straightened up.

"Well," Louise said. "Take a bow. You were right. He's a rotten bastard."

Becky shrugged.

"So, let me guess, you asked him for money and he's broke."

"Something like that, yeah," said Louise, surprised. "How did you guess?"

"Some people never change," Becky said. "Come on, you're coming home with me. You can phone Celeste later. You're not in any shape to be charging around town trying to deal with people like Stephen. Let him dig his own grave and rot in it."

"Becky, I was awful. I yelled at him. I was … I was right out of control. I even lied … told him I was going to go to school."

"Yeah? Jeez, maybe you are finally getting some sense. Good for you. C'mon, we'll take my car."

In all the years of their friendship, Louise had never been invited to Becky's trailer. Becky always showed up on her doorstep or met her in town.

The interior of the trailer was vibrant with colour. Becky had covered the walls with bright fabric and the floor with brilliantly patterned rugs. One window was stained glass. There were framed paintings on the walls and there were stained glass lamps with smoothly polished driftwood bases. Bookcases stuffed with books, magazines and file folders lined the walls. The small dining room table was of finished oak and had matching chairs. There was a daybed instead of a couch, with brown velvet cushions and carved curled armrests on the ends. There was a small elegant table covered with a silk scarf, holding three eagle feathers, an abalone shell, a polished white stone, a framed photograph of the moon. Louise stood in the doorway, shaking, trying to take it all in.

Becky handed her a nightgown and towels.

"Get in the shower," she said gently, "and stay there for a while. Then come and curl up on the bed. I'm putting on the electric blanket and making tea and chicken soup. And don't bloody argue with me and tell me you're okay. You're not."

When Louise emerged from the shower, the trailer was empty, but the teapot was steaming gently on the small inlaid table beside the bed, along with a bowl of homemade soup, toast, cheese and a jar of homemade jam.

She poured the tea, curled up under the warm blanket into a clenched circle on the bed and took a few small bites of toast. Flames licked at the space behind her eyes. She sat up and grabbed a book from the bookcase. Some environmental stuff. She searched the bookcase for something more distracting, but Becky was a serious reader. The blurbs on the book jackets made no sense. The letters blurred and danced in front of her. She wrapped her arms around herself. She felt sick. The food lay like cold stones in her stomach.

The door rattled. She unwrapped her arms and tried to look normal, but it didn't work. Becky sat down beside her. "It's okay," she said. "I just had to talk to Ma and I called Celeste. She knows where you are. I won't leave you again. You're in shock. That's why you need to eat and stay warm. You need someone to look after you for a bit so you don't have to do anything or go anywhere. Everything will take care of itself. Just give it time. Now lie down and get warmed up."

"Becky," said Louise after a while, after a spoonful of soup which went, pleading, all the way to the bottom of an empty sad knotted place. "I didn't. You know I didn't. I didn't leave anything on. Stephen said I was forgetful, but I checked. I always checked. My Dad always said the house was a firetrap. He always unplugged everything and so did I. I always went back to check, just because I am forgetful. Becky, it didn't start that way and nobody gives a shit. Everyone thinks its just an old house, let it go. Who cares? Nobody cares."

"I do," said Becky, "and Celeste cares, and Harold, and Mark in his own way. My whole family cares, Lou. They think a lot of you. They always have. Oh yeah, even George called. Said he had an old trailer you could have. For nothing. You see, people like you. They care. They've been dropping stuff off at Cel's and here. You'll have enough old clothes to start your own junk shop. There's gonna be a dance at the community hall on Friday to raise some money. All the stores have jars in them with your name on the side. Even the bank has started a fund."

Louise stared at Becky, horrified. "Oh no," she whispered. "No, tell them not to. I don't know why they're bothering. I even managed to burn my own house down."

"It wasn't your goddamn fault," Becky said slowly. "I've been thinking. What if it was set?"

"Yeah," Louise closed her eyes. They stung. She squeezed them hard to keep them shut, to keep anything from leaking out. "I know, I've been thinking about that, but it's too crazy. Who around here is that much of a monster? And why would anyone burn my house? It doesn't make sense."

"They wouldn't have to be from around here."

"Becky, just leave it, okay? I can't deal with this tonight ... I don't know what to do. I don't even know what to think. It's going to take me some time to sort all this out."

They sat in silence together.

"You want anything else. Book? TV?"

"Maybe the TV."

They watched the colours flick and tangle on the television. Louise tried to watch, to lose herself in watching, but she couldn't. After a while, Becky went to bed. Louise lay there, watching the screen, the small flames of colour, the voices and pleading of people far away with other problems — other than hers. She dozed and jerked awake again, all the while begging for something other than this to be happening.

The fire erupted silently, leapt and danced with a terrible controlled energy, tethered to the ground by the house roots, which were sunk deep into the yard, tangled with the roots of apple and plum trees, walnut, cedar, maple, alder. Her mother smiled at her from the flames. Her father's eyes were reproachful. The leaves on the apple trees crisped and curled. The grass caught fire. The barn exploded. Stephen handed her fistfuls of dollars bills which crumbled to ashes. Her mother and father disappeared into the flames.

She woke and sat up. The trailer was silent. She could hear Becky breathing in the other room. She picked up the book she had grabbed earlier and tried to read, but the letters danced on the page. She lay back down, watched the bit of sky through the window. Tomorrow, she'd have to go back and look for the cat.

Chapter 13

In the morning light, Louise lay and studied the trailer. Becky got up and made coffee while Louise watched the play of light from the stained glass window. The trailer was near the river, which wept and rumbled and complained outside the curtained walls.

The coffee Becky made was fragrant, rich, redolent with chocolate and spice. They stared at each other over fragile china cups.

"But why?" Louise asked the sun-mazed morning. "Why would anyone want to burn down my house? It doesn't make sense. Even if it had something to do with Celia, I mean, how does burning down the house do anything? It's too crazy. I'm just paranoid. Aren't I?"

Becky said nothing for a while.

"I don't know," she answered finally. "I don't know either."

After the coffee, after Becky had made them perfect omelettes with tiny triangles of toast, Louise amazed herself. A thousand faraway fragments of her self wandered and wept and raged while she made a list and spent the day, methodically and desperately, checking things off.

She phoned another lawyer — someone Becky had heard of in the next town, sixty miles away — and got advice over the phone. The man was cheerful, helpful and efficient. Louise was amazed all over again. The lawyer promised to phone Stephen and get a settlement. He didn't seem to think it would be a problem. He promised to call her back within a few days and let her know if and when she could expect some money.

She phoned the fire marshall and asked him, hesitating, if there was some way he could investigate the fire further. She explained her habit of unplugging things. She said she wanted to know how it had started, for her own peace of mind. He promised to be out later in the day and to go over it again. He was polite but distant.

She phoned Mark and asked when he planned on going ahead with the logging. He sounded surprised, but said he and Harold had already started moving equipment out to the farm. She snapped at him that he might have waited for her to finally agree. There was only silence in response to this. Then she told him about the fire marshall and asked him not to touch anything. He snorted at her, and said disgustedly, "Ah, jeez, Lou, no one would set that old house on fire. What the hell are you thinking about?" But he didn't argue beyond that and she didn't bother to explain.

She phoned Celeste, who was hurt that she was staying at Becky's but cheered up when she promised to come for dinner soon, promised to take Celia riding, promised she was okay.

"Celeste," she said, finally, tired of making promises. "Now I want you to do something for me. I want you to take Celia somewhere and get her a good counsellor. Don't dick around with these idiots in town; get her someone good, someone professional, who knows what she's doing. Celia's really hurting, and if she doesn't find someone to listen to her, she's going to hurt for a long time. I believe her when she says she was set up. There's something rotten going on, and I don't know what it is, but get that kid some help. Now! Okay? Promise?"

She finally hung up the phone and, dazed and shivering, went outside and down the path to the river. The river was still at its winter low. It wandered between gravel banks, glinting in the spring sun. The buds on the cottonwoods were brown and fat and sticky. Pussywillows jutted on the willow whips, sifting golden pollen into the breeze.

For once, the river was no comfort. She wandered to the water and stared at it, at the green and brown rocks and the tiny jade algae streamers stretched by the current. Then she wandered back to the trailer and stared at the phone. Becky finally came to get her and together they walked across the yard to the big house for lunch. Marie folded Louise in her arms and urged her to eat. Louise barely tasted the food even though Marie had pulled out all the stops and made broccoli soup, tiny cream biscuits, fried bacon, ham and sausages, and offered pie, cookies and home-canned peaches for dessert.

After lunch, Louise went back to the trailer. She lay down on the bed and Becky came and pulled the blanket up over her shoulders. Louise buried herself under the blanket and closed her eyes. From far away, she could hear many sounds: the river, birds, the slow ticking of the furnace in the wall next to her head, cars on the road. The world wavered and shook like thin mist; she thought of all the things she ought to do, tried to picture herself doing them and, instead, began deliberately to dream her way back into herself: horses, herself on horseback, riding, riding, the smooth leather of the saddle, the smell of earth, the sky shedding light on her bare head, the saddle creaking, wrapped around the strong solid horse body beneath her, the strength of the horse's body coming up from beneath her, nothing else to think about, holding her up, carrying her along. She slept through the afternoon. Becky woke her for supper. Still groggy from sleeping, she ate, then sat up until late into the night, watching television.

The fire marshall phoned the next morning.

"Could have been set," he said. "It didn't start in the house, that much I can tell. But that's about all. I'm sending some stuff for tests. I'll let you know. In the meantime, don't disturb anything, eh?"

Louise got in the truck and drove to the farm. Mark and Harold had already started clearing the road up the mountain. Mark was felling the trees ahead of the Cat; Harold was pushing out stumps and piling them with the Cat. The machine squeaked, rattled, grunted and roared; the treads crunched and ground over the splintering granite. Although they had only been working for an hour, they had already made an impressive mess.

She left the truck and walked up the hill, lifting her legs in their heavy rubber boots and crawling over the downed tree trunks and the jagged, broken branches like bright yellow sparks. There was a slippery litter underfoot of mashed-together needles, bark, mud and crumbled granite.

Mark nodded at her and motioned her back out of the way of the tree he was about to fell. She went back down the hill and began pulling at the severed tree branches, hoisting them onto the pile of stumps that Harold was pushing together. Harold smiled and waved.

He stopped the Cat for a moment and motioned her over. "Nice day, eh?" he said as he leaned down and handed her a pair of work gloves. "Good day for workin' … guess we'll get a start on 'er … finally. 'Bout time."

Louise nodded. Harold seemed to want to say something more but instead he grinned at her; the Cat jerked back into motion, and she went back to the branches.

They worked steadily all morning. Around eleven, Harold shut down the Cat, went down to his truck and fetched a thermos, a couple of plastic cups and a bag of cheap store-bought gingersnaps. The three of them sat together on a rock in the sun, Louise between the men. Solicitously, they made her take one cup and shared the other. The warm, male smell of grease and sweat radiated from them — a gentle, reassuring, familiar stink which blended with the heat from their bodies. The black coffee was bitter and hot; it mingled perfectly with the bite of the stale gingersnaps.

"Boy, that Jonsered, sure beats that piece a shit you used to have, eh," said Harold.

"Yeah," said Mark. "Damn thing. Choke went, then the clutch. One thing after another … had the parts for it, eh, had another old one, but you know, you can only fix a thing so many times. Naw, this is a good little saw … got a deal, gloves, kit, box, the whole shebang. Got her down at Pete's."

"Yeah, good saws at Pete's. Pricey though. Heard you could get the same damn thing for half price just by driving Stateside an hour or so and goin' to that new wholesalers, eh? Out on the freeway?"

"No shit, eh?"

Louise drank coffee and listened to them talk. They finished the coffee, silently stood up, tossed the coffee dregs at a bush and went back to their machines. Louise sat for a while longer by herself. Then she too, went back to hoisting the heavy branches onto the increasingly huge pile.

They worked for another couple of hours, broke from work and went to Celeste's for lunch, then came back and worked some more. After lunch, Louise had wanted nothing more than to keep sitting in the kitchen with Celeste, but she went with the men.

In the afternoon, she got tired. It was a lot harder work than pruning. For what seemed like hours, Louise stooped down, gathered armloads of pungent dead fir, hoisted the heavy wet branches onto the huge pile of stumps towering over her head. The gloves were sweaty and hot; she took them off. Then the fir stained her hands with the smell of old Christmases. As the afternoon wore on, she kept stopping to listen, imagining that from very far away she heard someone — a child perhaps — crying. But when she stopped to listen carefully, she knew it was only the the thin high squealing of the Cat — some piece of machinery grating against another. Whenever she really stopped to listen and pay attention, the noise blended with all the other noises, but still it got on her nerves.

She knew she had let Mark convince her that she was doing the right thing. This was normal, this is what people — real people, men — did.

They didn't get foolish over a few trees that would grow back. They cut
and tore up the earth and it was all for a good reason; it was no more
than good farming. Look at the bare fields below — they had once been
full of trees, before the pioneers came and changed everything. Pioneers did this without a choice; they cut and carved and demanded a
space for themselves. It was what all of her ancestors had done since
they had stopped wandering and settled on the land. When Mark cut
down the giant pine she had sat under so many days of her life, and
when Harold carved a road over the lip of the granite, unsettling
boulders which crashed and leapt down the hill and finally came to rest
in the gully by the road, she turned away and worked harder. What the
hell. What good had sitting under trees ever done her?

    When Harold and Mark finally packed their tools, parked the Cat
and drove down the road, she stood by the jagged yellow base of the
stump. It was still oozing bright globs of pitch, like clear fat. She looked
at it, then walked down through the lengthening dusk to the pasture
where the horses grazed and the killdeers ran away crying, crying their
wild evening cry all over the field. The horses came and nosed at her
for treats. She leaned against them, scratching their necks. She brought
them some hay they didn't really need, and they nosed at it then stood
beside her, snuffling gently at her through their noses in the hopes of
better food they might have missed, pulling and lipping at her coat and
hands until they got bored and moved away. She remembered she had
been going to look for the cat, and wandered along the fence line and
back around by the barn, calling. There was no sign of the cat.

    In the thickening light, the place where the house had been was a
huge hole in the sky — a gap in the strip of light along the mountains
that still held a vestige of the day. She couldn't bring herself to walk past
where it had been. Instead, she walked the long way up through the
corner of the pasture fence and back along the road to her truck.

    She looked towards the glow in the sky from the distant lights of
the town. "I'm not dead, you bastards," she said aloud. "I'm not dead.
I'm still alive." The air was warm on her face. Geese and swans called
and squabbled from the swamps far below the house, down by the river.
She kept listening. Very tentatively, the first frog of the season let out a
surprised few croaks and then fell silent. The killdeers went on crying,
crying to the dark. When she was a girl, that had been her favourite
sound.

    She stood on the road a long time, thinking that she might walk
down the trail through the trees to the swamp, and then across to the

river. The beaver might be out; she could sit quietly by the river in the
dark for a long silent while before going back to Becky's and to Marie's
and the crowded noisy house for dinner, with Marie pressing her, very
kindly, to eat a bit — just a bit — more.

Then she remembered Becky saying how much her Mom became
irritated when someone didn't show up for dinner on time. It must be
almost six by now. She climbed in her truck and, driving a bit too fast,
headed back down the hill.

Chapter 14

"Dinner and dance tonight," Becky said the next morning. "Don't forget. I gotta go to town but I'll be home in time to take you. Find something in the closet you want to wear. Everybody's coming. Might be fun."

"No way," said Louise. "I'm not going."

"Yeah, you are," Becky said cheerfully. "People want to help out and you're gonna let them, you old stiff-necked farmer. You'll just have to humble yourself."

"It'll be horrible," said Louise. "No one will come anyway, and if they do, it'll just be for an excuse to gossip."

"Oh, bullshit," said Becky. "You're just too damn sensitive. And you always expect the worst. Hey, sorry, I gotta go. Meeting someone for coffee, grease and sugar at the bakery. Couldn't miss such a delectable treat now, could I?"

Louise drove to where Mark and Harold were working. She stared at the pile of logs lying in the mud. Then she bent to pick up sticks and branches. But everywhere she turned, she was in the way. Harold leaned down from the Cat and yelled, "We'll do that later, Lou. Shovel it up with the blade."

Mark was up ahead somewhere. She could hear the saw whining, then it would pause and a tree which had been circling unsteadily, like a drunk coming out of the bar, would lean farther and farther, gain speed, hit the ground with a whump. Then silence.

She went to find Mark. He had lit a fire in one of the piles of branches, left it to smoulder. With a little coaxing, she made it burn, piled on green branches which sizzled, dried and exploded until the fire was a hungry pyre shooting sparks and light and heat into the gray spring sky.

When she drove home, covered in pitch and ashes, Becky greeted her with armloads of clothes to try, suggestions for jewelry and an offer from her sisters to do Louise's hair. Louise got herself into the shower and then into an almost-too-small maroon velvet dress. Then she took it off again.

"I can't," she said. "I feel stupid."

Becky sighed and went across the yard to consult. She came back with black tailored pants that fit, a white sweater and a white jacket. Showered, dressed, made up, her hair done, Louise was loaded in the car along with the food, some children, flowers for the hall decorations and the rest of the family.

Arriving at the tiny community hall was a shock. Normally the old log building, located just three miles from where her house had been, was hardly noticeable behind a screen of cedar trees. Tonight there were lights strung across the yard, cars pulling in, people Louise knew stopping in the parking lot to shake her hand and carrying in trays, platters, bowls, loaded with sliced turkey, ham and roast beef, salads, pickles and cheese, mashed potatoes, cookies, cakes, pies. Inside, the kitchen was full of women with aprons. Other women were setting long rows of tables and men were standing in the corners, uneasy in suit coats or stoking the huge wood stove in the corner.

People grabbed Louise's hand, shook it, murmured, "such a shame" and "how are you doing," and "let us know if there's anything more we can do" and went away. Most of them she recognized as friends of her parents or people she had sort of known all her life — neighbours she rarely spoke to, people who smiled and said hello at the mail box in the morning before going their own way, getting on with their lives.

Louise sat with Becky's family. They took up three tables. More people came by, more friends of her parents or people who lived along her road whom she knew only to speak to. They, too, shook her hand, went away and put money in the gallon pickles jars that stood on a table at the back of the room. Celeste and Harold arrived, and Mark and Janet with their boys. Tables filled up. Someone put country music on the scratchy sound system.

Harold and Celeste had brought all of their kids. The older kids disappeared and sat with friends. Louise patted the chair beside her, motioned to Celia. Celia sat down. She didn't look at Louise. She sat with her head down, not looking at anyone in the room.

"How's school?" Louise asked.

"Okay," Celia mumbled. She twisted her hair around her fingers.

They lined up for dinner. Louise chewed, swallowed, listened to conversations, said "yes," and "no," automatically, let her eyes roam the room. She counted heads: There were almost eighty people. She wouldn't have guessed that she knew eighty people.

"How did it start?" people asked her, over and over and over. "Do they know yet how it got started? Jeez, what a shame. Beautiful old place."

"Not yet," Louise answered and answered. "Not yet; no idea; not really, no, I don't think it was the wiring; no, not rebuilding, not for a while anyway; yes, it was awful. Yes, no, I don't think so." It was easier than she had thought it would be.

After dinner, groups of people went to the kitchen and washed dishes and others pushed the tables back. Rock music replaced the country music on the sound system. Then a group of people from the local evangelical church set up mikes and played hymns set to rock music. Their leader exhorted people to help "our sister in need."

Luckily, it all petered out fairly soon, just as Louise began to wonder when she could leave. The band played the few numbers they knew, then packed up and the sound system came back on. People began to leave, coming up to Louise to say goodbye. She smiled and smiled, until finally, mercifully, it was time to go.

Chapter 15

"Celia hates me," said Celeste. She was stomping around the kitchen, flinging dishes into the sink.

"No, she doesn't," Louise said. "Everyone says teenagers are difficult. So, she's difficult. She acts like she hates everybody."

"I'm going to write a book," Celeste announced. "All the bullshit they don't tell you in prenatal class. Like, the little-known fact that cute babies turn into hideous evil teenagers. Drown them at birth. Don't take a chance. "

"So, what's she done now?"

"She hates me. She even told me she hates the way I eat; she hates my clothes, she hates my hair, for God's sake. I can't do anything right. She hates our house, she hates my poor old car — which, God knows, is ugly, but hey, it moves and it gets us around. She hates the town, says she wants to move away."

"What about Harold?"

"Naw, she doesn't hate him. He never hassles her, never tries to make her do her homework or wear something other than torn tee-shirts and jeans and a ton of makeup, or wash her hair, or talk about her feelings or do something more than watch music videos. Jeezus, I am so fed up."

Savagely, Celeste dumped old coffee grounds into the sink on top of the dishes, poured more coffee into the machine, poured in water and snapped the machine on.

"So what did I do wrong?" she continued. "Oh, I only cook and clean and do a million tons of laundry and try to make a little money on the side and try to keep this family from falling apart at the seams. Who the hell am I to criticize her or say anything about anything? What the hell do I know?"

"Maybe she really is angry," Louise ventured.

"About what?" Celeste shouted. "We've done everything we could for her. We went to court and begged and pleaded and promised to be the best and strictest parents this world has ever seen so she could get off with a few community hours. Since then, I've trotted her off to counsellors, like you and everybody else said I had to. I've driven her to do the damn community hours and hung around town wasting time so I could drive her home again. I watch her like a hawk. I even volunteered to chaperone the school dance, so she could go and I could keep an eye on things. And if you think four hours listening to that screaming music is a joke, just go ahead and try it."

"Maybe she's angry because you and everyone else thinks she's a criminal."

"And you don't?"

"I just don't know. We don't know enough. If she'd just tell us who gave her the stuff and where it came from originally, maybe we'd have a chance to figure out the real story."

"Yeah, and even if we did, what difference would it make? So, you believe that cock and bull story she told you? The counsellor says she's in denial. The cops say she's just another juvie. Oh, yeah, the counsellor told me the whole thing is probably our fault anyway. She seems to think it has something to do with Harold's grandmother."

"What?"

"Yeah, you know — things like this run in families. That's what they used to think in the olden days. Well, guess what, things haven't changed much — just the language. Harold's grandmother was the crookedest old bootlegger you ever saw. Used to run a still in the brush behind her house. Harold said she used antifreeze to give her booze a special flavour. They used to believe in the old days that you could inherit bad genes, and now they've reinvented the same stupid idea, only it has some fancy new name — family systems or something. So, you see, no problem: Celia is just taking after her great-grandmother. Should have expected it."

"Oh, for God's sake, Cel."

"Naw, it's true. Actually, I don't think these sessions are doing us much good. I think we're going to try someone else."

"Celeste, we've got to get her to talk. It's the only way I can see."

"Yeah, sure, great. You go right ahead and try. You have my permission. Only don't come running to me if she bites your head off. It's not my problem."

"Tell her I'll be here at ten o'clock Saturday morning to take her riding."

"Make it noon. She never moves until then."

"Ten. Tell her."

"I dunno," Celeste said slowly. "I don't think the horses mean that much to her anymore. Not like they used to. Remember she used to nag and nag Harold to get her a horse. We always thought we'd wait until she got a bit older and a little more responsible. Maybe we shoulda got it. Maybe she wouldn't be in this mess now if we had."

Celeste's face sagged. Louise shrugged, impatient. "Bullshit. Don't start second guessing yourself, Cel, or you'll never stop. We gotta keep going somehow. Get out of this mess. All we can do is keep plugging. There's got to be a way out somewhere. Things have got to get better. They sure as hell can't get much worse."

They sat in silence.

"Come and see my crocuses," said Celeste. "I planted a whole huge bunch last fall, and are they ever pretty. Should be daffs pushing up any day now, too."

Saturday was sunny. Louise got up early, went to the farm, caught the horses and brushed them. Clouds of sneezy, itchy dust and hair flew off their backs and floated in the sunshine. She fetched the saddles from the barn. At least they hadn't burned up in the fire.

Actually, she thought, the only thing she really missed now was the house itself. There hadn't really been that much in it of value. Old furniture, clothes, photographs, her stereo. But she already had been given two other old stereos, clothes and enough worn-out furniture to stock a small second hand store. Other people's junk was easy to come by. She could have her own garage sale if she wanted, now that she seemed to have everyone else in the neighbourhood dumping their castoffs on her. No, that was mean.

Becky was right. People had been generous. The day after the dinner and dance she had stood, her face bright with heat, in the kitchen of Becky's trailer and accepted the envelope full of five- and ten- and twenty-dollar bills from the evangelical minister and two large smiling women in flowered dresses — people she didn't know and whose church she had never considered attending. It was equally humiliating that they were people who still, somehow, couldn't see her, even after shaking her hand at the dinner. But there was still a jar at the corner store with her name on it and more bills in it.

Celia was actually waiting for Louise, her face a stormy sullen mask.

Louise ignored her, swept cheerfully into the kitchen, downed two cups of coffee in a row and swept out again, dragging Celia with her. Celia huddled in the corner of the truck cab and closed her eyes.

When they arrived at the farm, Celia stumbled from the truck like an ancient drunk, slouching across the ground to lean limply against George, her favourite horse. He turned his head to nose and lick at her hands. Celia petted him and mumbled something, making no move to help, while Louise saddled both the horses, silently cursing to herself. She could sympathize wth Celeste if this is what she put up with all the time.

Louise got on Bigger, her favourite horse. He was a big jugheaded bay with a stubbornly cheerful attitude towards things. He liked going up mountains and bulldozing his way through brush and staying ahead of George; and he liked coming back down towards home. George was different. He always shied and jigged sideways as they were leaving, trying to make excuses so they'd all stay home. But once they were out away from the farm, he pulled hard, trying to get in front of Bigger, flirting his tail and jumping sidways in mock horror at strange-looking bushes and stumps. But Celia had never minded his idiocy in the past. She thought George was fun and Bigger was dull.

Today, the horses both moved out readily, ears pricked, shying a little at the strangeness of new scents on the familiar road. "Boy, they're glad to get out for a change, eh?" Louise called to Celia. "Been a long winter for them, too. I can't remember the last time I took them out. Must have been before it got really cold."

Celia didn't answer. She was huddled over George, looking cold.

"Oh, for Chrissakes," Louise snapped. "This is supposed to be fun, not a goddamn punishment. Sit up and get off his back. You know better than that. First ride of the spring, his back is going to be soft."

Celia reluctantly straightened up, but her sullen expression didn't change. Louise wondered in despair if this was going to be simply a long, dull ride — maybe a last ride together, another chip out of what remained of their friendship.

They rode up an old logging road, Celia lagging behind. Louise headed towards a high ridge where there was a good spot to stop for a breather.

Hooves clattered behind her. Celia flashed by at a gallop and Bigger, startled, lunged awkwardly into a gallop as well. Louise swore out loud. It was a strict rule on rides that no one took off without warning and agreement from the other riders. She'd taught Celia that — taught her all the rules and enforced them.

She pushed Bigger to keep up, and he responded; she came up just behind Celia and yelled angrily, "Hey, slow down, what do you think you're doing?"

Celia didn't answer, but George's pace slowed to a fast canter. Side by side, they rocked up the hill to where the path began to narrow into a passage between thick trees. Louise pushed Bigger in front of George and pulled him down to a trot and then a walk, so that George was forced to slow as well.

They stopped at the top of the hill and Louise turned in the saddle to face Celia. "That was stupid," she said. "You know better than that. And you know better than to run George in front. What if he'd shied and dumped you? Plus it's too rocky here to gallop. What the hell were you thinking about?"

Silence from Celia. Grimly, Louise waited.

They sat there. The horses puffed and sweated, moved uneasily, still wanting to run some more. Louise gave up, started to pick up Bigger's reins. They might as well go home and write the morning off as a lousy time, a failed attempt at communication.

"Louise," said Celia. "What do you think happens when people die?"

Louise stared. "Damned if I know," she said.

"But what do you think?"

Louise stared outwards at the mountain rippling down towards the blue valley bottom. What did she think?

"I guess," she said, "the most I can figure out, is we come from all this, we're made from it all: the earth, the river, the trees, the sky, the stars. We're part of it, somehow, and when we die, we go back to it — molecules, energy, something like that."

"But have you ever thought about what it would be like, dying?"

Louise shifted in the saddle. This conversation had an edge that worried her.

"Sure," she said. "Everyone thinks about it, even when they try not to. I don't worry about it too much ... although I remember when I was a kid, I worried about it a lot. I used to worry that my Mom or my Dad would die and leave me and Mark behind. Sometimes, I tried to figure out which one I could most stand to be without, Mom or Dad. Talk about a dumb question. Why, honey? What have you been thinking about? What's put these weird ideas into your head?"

"Nothing," said Celia. "I've just been wondering." Louise waited but Celia didn't volunteer anything more.

They turned the horses to start back down the hill. But Celia wasn't quite finished.

"Remember that guy?" she said. "That kid I told you about. The one who gave me the drugs?"

"Yeah," said Louise.

"He had some pills," Celia said matter-of-factly. "Said he could kill himself anytime he wanted, just by taking one of them. He showed them to us. Said anytime one of us wanted some, just let him know. He cut his wrists once too, he said, but I didn't see that. He has all these scars on his arms. He's weird but nice too, sort of."

Louise went cold all over.

"Celia," she said. "That's a lousy thing to think about. You ever, ever try something like that, your Momma would come after you and kill you all over again and so would I. Get any such stupid ideas out of your head, right now."

"Mom wouldn't give a shit," Celia said. "She thinks I'm a juvie drug taker, anyway."

"Celia, she does not! She loves you totally. She'd do anything for you."

"The only person who listened to my side was you. And even you don't believe me."

"I do believe you. And I told your mother I believe you. But I wanted you to tell me the whole story so I could try and do something to help. I need to know who gave your friend the stuff."

Celia turned and looked her in the eye. "I didn't want to tell you because I thought you'd be really mad."

"At what?"

Celia sighed deeply, a long shuddering breath that went all the way down to her toes.

"It was some guy — that friend of Stephen's, the one who was there one time when I came by with Mom. I don't know his name."

"Friend of Stephen's? What friend of Stephen's?"

"Dunno. I think he works in an office."

"Office? What office? What does he look like?"

"A man. I dunno. With a suit. And a pot belly. He was at your house one time when I was there. Please, don't tell anyone I said anything. Okay? Please?"

"Okay," said Louise slowly, "I'm not going to say anything. I promise. You've been through enough. You know what I'd really like?" she said fiercely. "I'd like to forget all this shit for just a little while and just have fun, and go riding like we used to, and play and be goofy. Wanta try?"

"Yeah," said Celia. "Yeah, let's."

They grinned at each other. Louise's heart lifted. She felt better than she had for a long time, even as dread about Stephen nagged and nagged, a hidden sharp flash of fear. What was Stephen's role in all this, and why hadn't he said anything?

They turned the horses again, went back up the road, came to a stretch where there was room for a canter and rocked along side by side until the horses were blowing. The wind in Louise's face lifted her hair and her spirits. On the way home, Celia told her bad jokes from school and they laughed together. They unsaddled and brushed the horses together.

When Louise brought Celia home, Celia, for once, swept into her mother's arms and hugged her. She even hugged her little sister and then went yelling and singing up to her room. Louise reported to Celeste that they had, for sure, had a good day.

Celeste demanded Louise stay for dinner and tell her every detail, but she made a whole string of excuses and left. She wanted time, for God's sake — time alone, just for a while; time without disasters or consoling friends or sinking thoughts of her ex-husband. Maria wouldn't be expecting her for dinner. She'd assume that Louise was at Celeste's.

With immense relief, Louise drove back to the farm. Feeling like a kid sneaking out of some duty, she took the path down to the river, almost running down the hill, balancing her way acroos the fallen logs over the swamp, past the bitter, rankly fertile smell of swamp cabbage; the frogs fell silent as she came and started up again behind her as she left, as she went plunging into the dark woods like a child under a favourite blanket — for a short brief while hidden, disconnected and alone.

A blue heron, almost invisible, squawked sadly away across the water as she came up to it. The water glimmered and talked to itself. Louise sat down on the bank; the cold wet mud sank into the seat of her jeans.

"Susan," she thought. "Susan, Susan, Susan, Susan." If Susan were here, if Susan were here … she buried her head on her arms and waited, absolutely still and silent, as if waiting were the only thing left to do. She grabbed her arms with her hands and held on, digging in her fingers.

After a long while, she opened her eyes. The water at her feet was utterly black; only the sky above the trees still held a trace of light. She pushed herself over to the edge of the bank and waited. Coldness drifted upwards from the water onto her face.

"You're a coward, Louise," she said out loud. "You never make decisions. You can't handle your life and you're too chicken to die." The woods around her were black and silent.

"But I don't want to die," she thought. "I just don't want to live — not this hard, not this way, not anymore. I want Susan ... or someone. I want my own house. I want my own money. I want my own life."

The water looked as thick as molasses, unmoving. From inside this thickness there were odd rustles and murmurings, tiny slitherings and faint splashes. The cottonwood trees clicked and shivered.

She stood up and walked along the bank to where the cattle had made a trail down to the water. She slid down the trail and stepped onto what looked like a sandbar. As soon as she stepped on it, she realized her mistake. The river was lowering itself daily, leaving mudbanks exposed to the air. She stepped back as soon as her foot sank into the ooze, but there was no purchase for her other foot and it sank as well. The mud was the temperature of ice and bit harshly through her socks and running shoes.

Shit, she thought. What a pain. I'll show up at Becky's wet and covered in mud and she'll think I'm an even bigger fool than ever.

Carefully, she tried to pull one foot free, but it was sunk up to her calf. The other was behind her, which threw her weight off balance. When she tried to pull up her front foot, the rear foot sank just as deeply. Neither would budge; she couldn't move. She'd seen cows stuck like this. The suction got their legs and if they weren't pulled out, they lay in the mud and died. The thick cold mud wrapped itself around her legs, squeezing. Her legs began to burn and then to ache, fiercely. She tried again to move and only sank deeper. Shit, she thought desperately. What am I going to do? What she needed was a pull, a lever, something to get her weight up and off her feet.

She twisted herself, leaning sideways, feeling in the dark, trying to get her hands on something solid — the bank, a stick, an overhanging branch, anything. She remembered what her father had said about this kind of mud: river mud, silty mud. Every summer, the farmers who ran cows down here lost a few head to it. "The more you move around, the worse it gets," he had said. "Kinda turns to jelly. Gets a skin on it when it's dry so's you can walk on it. Under the skin, just brown soup."

The light had now gone entirely and she could barely see. Her hands were white glimmers in front of her face. She tried to reach, to keep feeling with her hands while keeping her legs still. Her legs felt like they had been set into freezing solid concrete.

The solidity of the river bank was only inches away, directly behind her rear foot — if only she could figure some way to get a purchase on it. There was also a faint outline, a denser shade of black, ahead of her, which might be a log or just a tangle of branches and old grass.

"I could die here," she thought, "alone in the dark …" They'd find her eventually, but not in time. No one came down here until summer, and then just a few fishermen. She'd slide down under the mud and disappear. No one would ever know what had happened, the mud filling her mouth, her nose, her eyes. Desperately, she jerked at one foot then the other and only sank deeper.

"Goddammit," she thought desperately. "This is too much. This is too goddamn ridiculous, stuck here in a swamp like a stupid cow. No way. I am damned if I'm going to die here."

She heaved herself forward and stretched out until one hand made purchase on the black outline: a log — a small one, old and slimy, covered with moss. Something broke under her hand and she scrabbled with her fingernails. She was flat on her belly in the sour reeking mud, until she could get the other hand on the log as well and, inch by inch, drag herself towards it, pulling her feet and legs from the sucking mud.

She got her knees on the log and balanced herself there, peering through the black, trying to determine where the actual solid shore might be. She'd have to jump and chance making it or landing in more mud. Very carefully, she stood up on the skinny log, which rocked in the now-liquid mud and began to sink. She balanced, holding out her arms, and gathered herself, waiting, remembering how she and Mark had done it — climbing in the barn or walking across logs over ravines in the mountains. Wait until your body knows, until your body feels sure. That's what they had learned.

Without thought or effort, she sprang for the bank, landing on her hands and knees. Solid ground, grass.

Only now was she aware of the night sounds around her — the crickets and frogs, the geese far away in more open water, the curlews still running and crying in the dark.

She went back up the hill with quick sure steps, feeling her way in the dark, but knowing, all the way, where she was, blessing the solidity of dry soil. When she made it back to the truck, she tried to wipe some of the mud off herself, but it was plastered in thick, sticky flakes which clung and then fell onto the floor of the truck as they dried.

Chapter 16

"**B**ecky, I just figured something out."

Louise and Becky were lying side by side on the fold-out bed in Becky's trailer. The television was on but the sound was muted. Louise was wrapped in one of Becky's nightgowns; they were drinking hot chocolate and eating popcorn soaked in butter, cayennne pepper and garlic powder.

Louise thought she really ought to be trying harder to find some other place to stay — she was taking advantage. Becky must be getting tired of her by now, must want back her space and privacy.

"Yeah, what'd you figure out?" Becky was watching the television.

"Well, I was standing there in the mud and even though it probably wasn't that dangerous, it felt dangerous. It was dark and I couldn't see anything and no one knew where I was."

"Yes, it was dangerous, you idiot," Becky exploded. "Jeezus, Louise, you ought to know that. Those mudholes are scary places."

"But I wasn't really scared. It just felt like I might die there — like I could, like I had a choice. It would have been easy. All I had to do was nothing, just stand there and sink. And then I decided not to die. So I crawled out. I can't even remember exactly what I did. Just sort of heaved and wriggled."

"Yeah, so …?"

"That's the point. I decided."

Becky just looked, lifted one eyebrow and waited.

"That's it, the whole thing. I guess I never realized, I never felt it, that I had a choice. I mean, before. And I decided. No one else. No one made me. It wasn't a big deal. It's just … I figured out that I can decide something."

Becky snorted. "Yeah, that's the big one, all right. Deciding. And then living with what you decide. Took me years to figure that out. Still haven't quite got it."

Louise lay back on the pillows. Becky had heaped the bed with pillows — warm pillows in many-coloured fabrics. Becky's leg was solid against hers. Except for the foolish flickering television, the room was dark. Becky breathed and ate and the sound of popcorn was loud in the room. Louise left her leg there, let it lay still with the warmth going back and forth and her heart clamped like a steel lid on the knowledge of Susan and what was possible and what was not. She lay very quiet and Becky turned her head and smiled and … no, that wasn't it … or Louise got up from the bed and left, fled into the night with the remnants of loneliness and dignity wrapped around her like a black cloak … but, no, that wasn't it either. What she had was here, with Becky smiling at her, a little puzzled … and she had only to move her hand a little distance, only to turn her head, and … what would happen next? Louise turned over, moved her leg away from Becky's, pushed her face in the pillow, yawned — made it normal.

"Must be bedtime," she said, saying anything so long as it was banal, broke the moment, sent her tumbling back down into the dim normal room full of blue light. More than anything, she wanted to get up, put on her clothes, walk outside into the night, into the lost, cold, pure and lonely night, where she would be the only one: the one seeing in the dark, the one hiding, the one unseen; the one lost. Left. The one not cared about. The one who needed no caring. It was an answer. It was a choice.

"You tired?" Becky inquired kindly. "Guess I'll go to bed, too. See you in the morning, kid. Keep on deciding. You're doing okay."

Louise lay still for a long time with her eyes open, fixed on the dim square window. There was a place in her like a glass bowl, shattered and lying on the floor in pieces. If she could find all the pieces, she would have to find glue, then fit and twist and put it all back together. But the pieces would never fit. And she would never find the pieces.

She thought that perhaps, in the morning, she would call the lawyer again, even though he would think her a nuisance. He had called, once, sounding cheerful, but with nothing concrete to report.

She knew what she needed to do, and she didn't want to do any of it. She had to identify Stephen's fat friend. She had to find out about this teenage boy with the slashed wrists and pockets full of pills. She had to pick up these shards — these bright, razor-sharp bits of glass stuck in her flesh, in her life. Celia wanted her to do it. Celia needed her to do it. And so did Celeste.

Stephen: once her husband; once her man; once someone she kissed goodnight. His lips were thin; his chin always slightly bristling. He smelled of cigarette smoke and sweat and aftershave. He was unlike Susan, who smelled of pine needles, warm leaves, sunshine, apricots.

But Stephen was a lawyer. He wouldn't get involved with anything illegal. Or would he? Did she really know him? She turned over in the bed, kicked at the covers; she was too hot, it was too hot in the trailer.

If she could go home to her own house on a night like this, she'd give up trying to sleep, get up, maybe brew a pot of tea, sit by the window watching the stars and the horses moving under them. She would thinking about everything. Her old cat would come and sit at her feet. The cat was still gone. She had kept on looking for it, asked the neighbours, with no success. She turned over, kicked, turned again, wrapped the blankets around her shoulders, kicked them off her feet. Becky snored on in the other room.

Tomorrow, Louise decided, tomorrow she would get control of her life. She tried to arrange it all in her head: call the lawyer. That was the first thing. She had to get some money and then she could decide what came next — whether to move away or start trying to figure out how to build a new house. If she moved away, she could finally go to school. And take what? That had always been her problem. She'd tried lots of things. Nothing had ever moved her as much as the sight of the emerald, springing grass in April under the wooly apple trees; nothing moved her like the smell of earth after rain, the taste of a Gravenstein apple picked up from under the tree as she walked across the yard in September to where the horses stood, drowsy, heads over the fence, waiting for her. She could have been — still could be — a social worker, a teacher, a bureaucrat, a woman in a suit and good shoes. She could be in an office, in a suit, with a paycheque and a briefcase; or she could be lazy, sit under an apple tree with her mouth open, waiting for something to fall on her head and wake her from dreaming: dreaming of apples and apple trees, of playing in the mud, of the ripe smell of earth sucking down and devouring the desperate gray detritus left from winter.

No, she thought, school was what she needed; school was sensible, was right. If she went to school she could do something she had always

really wanted to do — learn and learn and learn, and find the answers
to her confusion; read and think about things and find people to talk to
about them.

And when she was done, when she came home, there would be her
empty yard and the decimated hillside above it, and no job. She would
be back to pruning apple trees. Why not — *if* she came home. Maybe
that wasn't such a bad idea — maybe a year or two would change her
enough, give her the breathing room, a chance to make some new
decisions. Maybe what she needed to do was see herself — her life, the
valley, the town — from the outside, from far away.

She tried to picture the process of actually leaving and saying
goodbye. She imagined herself getting on the bus and going away, over
the mysterious mountains on the long, thin blue road, going somewhere she'd never been, to a city full of strange people, finding a place
to live and getting things to keep herself alive — a kettle, a teapot, a
plant or two. She imagined going out and getting on busses and walking
through crowded filthy streets looking in the faces of strange people;
she imagined coming home with her books and her briefcase.

She could go to bars — to bars she'd heard about, read about —
and meet other women, women like her. But she didn't really want to
meet women, unknown women; she wanted to meet one woman, a
woman who would come towards her with a smile, take her hand, take
her home, or come home with her; someone who would walk through
the swamp and under the pine trees and ride George and Bigger.

But that wouldn't work either. It wouldn't work, none of it.

She turned again, bunching the pillow under her head and pulling
the blankets back over herself — too hot with them; too cold without
them. Tomorrow, for sure, she'd leave — at least, leave Becky's. She'd
stayed here long enough. She'd get a tent and at least move back onto
her own land. Maybe, there, she would be able to think more clearly.

Maybe it was, indeed, time to take control, stop dreaming, leave the
valley. Maybe a lifetime of pruning trees and gardening and living
hand-to-mouth wasn't worth it. Maybe she needed to do something
about the nagging irritable feeling that somewhere else there were
people doing things that meant something and that she knew nothing
about — people who knew and cared nothing about her, her life, her
foolish, foolish dreams. People who never would care. And why should
her dreams matter?

Irritably, she threw the covers back again, sat up and swung her feet
to the floor. She needed to make a list, to try and organize her chaotic

thoughts. She stood for a moment at Becky's door. She could still hear, unchanged, Becky's calm, even, gentle breathing.

She was tempted to look inside, to look on Becky's face in sleep, but instead she switched on the small lamp on the desk and sat on the chair. There was a jar of pens and pencils, scattered papers and a file of letters and bills. She leafed through the papers looking for some blank paper on which to write. There were letters and pleas for money from various organizations — women's organizations, environmental organizations.

She turned over some paper with close, scrawled writing and looked at it closely. It was Becky's handwriting; she knew it well enough from all the notes left on her door. She shouldn't read it, she thought, but then her eyes were caught by her own name, scrawled across the page.

"Louise is trying to figure out what's going on, who the crazy mafia dope dealers in town are ... hope she doesn't get hurt. I could tell her, I guess, but what good would it do? The sooner this all blows over, the better ..."

She scanned the rest of the letter; family news, emotional disclosures, the search for a job — familiar stuff. One page of a letter to somone she didn't know, but someone who obviously knew about her or why mention her at all? She turned over the rest of the papers. Nothing else there she didn't aready know. So even Becky, her trusted friend, knew something about this whole weird experience and wasn't telling her what it was.

Louise felt like she was back in high school, when everyone seemed to know some secret that she couldn't figure out. They knew how to do their hair; they knew the clothes that were popular. They knew secrets she wasn't privy to and had never been able to figure out. They knew the rules and how things worked. Even when school ended, they still knew all the right things: how to get jobs, big houses, nice marriages, perfect children; and after they got these things they knew how to keep them, how to defend them against other people — the ones who didn't know, like her.

She put the paper down, turned the light out and crawled back into bed. She felt astonishingly clear and sad. She had never wanted to be in this war, to kick and fight and scrabble her way to somewhere safe; but what else was there to do? First she had to figure out the rules. Someone, somewhere, knew how things worked.

Becky seemed to know something and didn't want to tell her. Susan had known the rules; that's why she had left before things got serious, before Louise could figure out a way to clutch on, to keep her enclosed and cozy in an ancient gray farmhouse. Which Susan would have hated.

She had let Susan walk away and was left, in her solitude, to be comforted by her grotesque lonely nobility; she was lonely and proud of her ability to withstand the loneliness, proud of her independence and the tiny enclosed security of the nest she had carved for herself in an alien world. And she had been, once, determined to stay in that nest.

Finally, briefly, she slept. In the gray morning, she got up before Becky and left without even making tea. She left a note beside the letter, which she had turned back over on the desk. She didn't want Becky thinking she'd read it, that she would do such a thing; but then again, Becky was smarter than that. She always figured things out.

Chapter 17

Louise drove to the town and had a sort of breakfast — several cups of tea and cold toast in one of the cafés. Her stomach turned over at the smell and sight of the toast. She ate out the greasy insides, left the crusts. The place was bright and noisy, with florescent lights, a radio, a giant flickering Coke sign over the counter and truck drivers taking a break, doing business over coffee and bacon and eggs and pancakes.

She finished her breakfast and went outside and down the street to the Outdoor store, but it was closed. She remembered, suddenly, that it was Sunday morning. Everything was closed. Her sense of time had stretched and thinned. Was it only yesterday that she had gone riding with Celia? Was it yesterday that she had become stuck in the swamp? How could she have forgotten it was Sunday morning?

Besides, she didn't really have enough money to buy a tent. She walked back to to the truck and drove to Stephen's house without stopping to consider what she was doing. She drove without thinking, making the familiar turns; the truck seemed to drive itself. She had the odd sensation that if she took her hands off the wheel, it would still turn and twist on its own.

The house itself looked quiet; but then, it always looked quiet. The curtains were drawn. She went up the walk, past carefully dug flower beds full of crocuses, daffodils and tulips just poking up green spiky leaves, and rang the bell. No one came for a long time and she stood on the steps watching the sun break through the clouds and light up the patches of fog down by the river. What kind of an idiot was she about to make of herself? From somewhere far away, she noticed she was shivering.

Finally, she heard footsteps and Stephen opened the door, still tying the belt of his dressing gown.

"Jeezus, Louise," he said, squinting. "It's Sunday morning. And it's goddamnmed early. What are you doing here? What's happened now?"

Behind him, coming down the stairs, was Bimbette from the office. She glared at Louise. Louise stared back and Bimbette dropped her eyes.

"I have to talk to you, Stephen. It's important."

"Tell your lawyer," he snapped. "That goddamn shyster has been on my case every day for the last week. Wants his share of the spoils. I told him Friday I'd settle out of court. You should hear from him Monday morning. Now leave me alone. You'll get your damn money. Okay?"

"Stephen, its not about that," she said. "It's about Celia."

He looked at her and then snapped at Bimbette, "Go make some coffee."

"Oh, all right. Come in, then," he said to Louise. He sighed heavily and gently, through his mouth, like a man patiently resigned to losing all hope of peace and quiet on an early Sunday morning. He pulled back the ornate heavy door and she went across the broad gray carpet into the living room, where she sat down on the wide, blue, velvety couch and twisted her ancient muddy running shoes in under her knees.

Stephen sat down in the overstuffed chair across from her and they looked at each other.

"Well," he said. "What the hell do you want?"

"Stephen," Louise said slowly, "Celia told me it was a friend of yours who gave those kids the drugs. It's that guy with the potbelly, what's his name, the one I never liked — Sam Edwards."

"What's that go to do with me?" he snapped.

Louise experienced the same sensation she remembered having when, as a kid, she had jumped from the barn rafters onto the high-piled hay. She closed her eyes for a second, then said, "Stephen, anyone can put two and two together. He's a friend. He's been here. You had to have known something. You should have told me, and you didn't. If I can figure that much out, so can other people. You're the one who always said there's no secrets in this place."

Then Stephen surprised her. He put his head in his hands and shook it back and forth, then he rubbed his face again, like a man waking from sleep and blinked very quickly several times. "What a mess," he said. "What a bloody mess."

Louise stared at him and she waited. She didn't know what was the best thing to say, so she didn't say anything.

"Look, I don't actually know how those kids ended up with the drugs," Stephen finally continued. He looked at her. His blue eyes; his familiar sandy hair. "I want you to know I had nothing to do with it. Yes, it's true, I do happen to know what happened but of course, I couldn't say anything before and I'm not going to tell you anything more now. Lawyer's privilege. You know all that stuff. I'm only sorry Celia got mixed up in it. But you know, she shouldn't have been there. Were you aware those kids had been drinking?

"Little spoiled brats," he added, after a moment. "You'd think their parents could try a little harder to keep them under control."

"So, then, what are you going to do about it? And why," Louise asked carefully, "does someone need you for their lawyer? No one's been charged but Celia. Have they?" She still wasn't sure what they were actually talking about.

"Sorry, that's all I can tell you. And nothing is what I'm doing," said Stephen. "I'm not doing a damn thing. I told you already, I don't have anything to do with this whole mess except as Sam's lawyer. There's nothing to be done anyway, nobody's ever going to prove anything. Except kids these days are even dumber than we were. So what the hell."

Bimbette appeared suddenly with coffee on a tray, flopped it down ungraciously on the coffee table and exited, flouncing. Louise watched her leave. As if she cared.

Then Louise's mind spun back to what Stephen had just said. Sam Edwards was one of those people who stuck around, stuck to things, had to be pried off people at parties. He was the last to go home, always wanting to stay, finish the wine, keep talking — a good old boy kind of salesman, deal-maker-know-it-all, big in the Chamber of Commerce, on several committees, friends with the Mayor ... although he never really seemed to have a business of his own. He was friendly, too friendly, with everyone — always on the lookout, the make, the edge. He had a reputation for all kinds of things, but none of the dirt floating around him stuck. She vaguely remembered that he'd been fired once, from some kind of contracting job with the municipality; something about missing funds. She had never heard any more about it and it never seemed to slow him down. He was always putting a deal together — real estate or investment, or something. He had come to Stephen's house a few times. He had soaked up beer like a sponge and, once, when she had to push past him in the hall, he had leered at her and said something obscene. But she hadn't paid any attention, because men were always that way when they were drinking and some men were worse than others. So: Sam Edwards.

"Stephen," she said. "This is not fun and games anymore, you know. Someone burned my house down. I got the fire inspector to come out again and he's sent stuff to the lab. And they're going to find out who did it." That probably wasn't true, she thought, but she might as well throw it in.

"Someone has got Celia and her friends scared to death. They're playing with the notion of suicide. Celia asked me what I thought about death. She said one of her friends had some pills."

Stephen didn't say anything. The silence stretched into thinness, like a rubber band stretched too far.

Louise stood up and went to the window and looked out. It was getting sunnier. The houses and lawns looked fresh-washed in the pale sun. She turned back to the room. "By the way, how much money are you giving me?" she asked.

"Thirty-five thousand," he said. "I'll have to mortgage this house to do it. I hope you're satisfied."

"Stephen, you make $120 an hour! How can you be short of money?" she demanded, shocked.

"Just take it, shut up and start minding your own business," he said. "It's the best I can do. You could probably get more if you sued, but I just don't have it, so forget it. Tell your shyster lawyer to back off and leave me alone."

"So that's it," she said. "I get the money; I shut my mouth and pretend I'm happy. It's not enough to replace my house and live on, but it's something. Celia gets to grow up and forget all about everything. Your pal Sam … yeah, I remember all about him … he leaves town, I guess. No more parties with the mayor, no more drinking buddies at the Chamber."

"He's an idiot," said Stephen. "This town would be better off without him."

Louise stared at her shoes. All kinds of words paraded across the movie screen in her head — old shoot-out scenarios, white hats and black hats, happy endings.

"What about the kids?" she said finally. "What about their lives? What about me? What about Celeste and Harold? What about little concepts like right and wrong? I know I'm stupid, Stephen. I don't know much about the world you live in and I'm not sophisticated and I don't know how to live right, but jeezus bloody hell, Stephen, how can you be such a slime ball and keep breathing? How do you look anyone in the eye anymore?"

"Don't whine," he snapped. "I hate whiners. You'll get your money. That's what you were after all along, weren't you? Now get lost. Go live out there on your hill in hillbilly heaven or do whatever you want to. Just leave me alone. Understand? No more. We're through, quits, you've got nothing on me, and I want nothing more to do with you."

Stephen stood up and went to the door. Louise forced her stiff legs to carry her back across the carpet and out the door and down the shiny concrete sidewalk to the truck. She got in and slammed the door, started the truck and drove back downtown to the bakery which, fortunately, was open at last. She went in, ordered tea with two huge sugary donuts and gulped them down. She drank the tea scalding hot but it didn't warm her up.

Numbly, she left the bakery and walked the block and a half to the RCMP station. She stood on the sidewalk, thinking. Stephen was right. She didn't know anything. She had a name — maybe; she had Celia's story, the fire at her house. Finally, she went and tried the door of the station. It was locked. A sign by the door said gave a number to be phoned in case of emergencies. The prefix was the number for the neighbouring, larger town.

"What am I going to do?" she said out loud.

She got in the truck and drove the long way back to her farm. All kinds of arguments raged in her head — things she could have said to Stephen; things she could say if she got the courage to the call the police. Once she slowed and almost stopped, but all she wanted to do was to get home, to get somewhere safe, to go somewhere she could think.

At the farm, she got out of the truck and stood in the yard. The horses nickered at her, only momentarily distracted from their grazing on new green grass. She watched them for a long time, then she got a three-legged picking ladder from the barn and her pruning shears from the truck and set the ladder up under one of the apple trees. She walked around the tree, looking at it, thinking perhaps it was too tall. She could take out the two largest branches on top. Then she went to work, skinning up the ladder and into the tree, shifting her weight from rung to rung and branch to branch. The trees weren't that bad. Her Dad had kept them pruned and she had pruned them the last few years. There were only a few tangles to cut out, but, for sure, the trees were too tall — the upper branches were now growing straight up, reaching for the sky. Even standing on the tallest branch that would hold her, stretching with the clippers, she couldn't reach. She slid back down for the pruning saw.

When she came back up, she clambered around the trunk, took out all the suckers first; then she climbed off the ladder and into the tree, up through its forks until she was balancing gingerly on the top branches. With the saw chewing a fast slide through the soft green wood, she cut off several of the tallest top branches. They crashed to the ground with satisfying viciousness. The trees were slippery with moss and she slipped and slid, too fast, from branch to branch, hooking an elbow and a knee or wedging a toe to hold herself, cutting with a steady, even rhythm that didn't stop to ask which cuts to make, the clippers an extension of her hands, her body an extension of the tree. She danced with it as a sloth might dance — a slow, even, steady ballet that moved her imperceptibly up and down and all around the tree — until, finally, she stood back, cocked a critical eye, walked around the tree and noted places where she might have taken more. But, as her father had always said, bringing back old trees took time, no point in rushing it. She propped the pruners in a branch and headed for the house for a cup of tea.

And stopped.

"No, no," she muttered slowly, sinking inexorably to the ground, pushed down by the knowledge that it really was gone: her house, her safety, her home, her refuge. And it wasn't just the house: it was her mother, turning to her, smiling, with a plate of cookies; it was her father, coming inside with his characteristic stomp, banging his boots to get the mud off, settling into his chair by the stove with a sigh and slowly unlacing his workboots — a sign that the day's work was over and he could relax.

It was her and her brother, racing up and down the stairs in some mindless game of tag or playing war with miniature plastic soldiers on rainy days, until he became too old for those games.

"Mark," she thought. "Mark, I want to talk to Mark." He was the only one who might — who could — fathom the extent of her loss, but he too had left her, had been taken away and disappeared into the world, the language, the code of men.

And now Stephen was gone as well — or, at least, the hope of Stephen; the thought, always at the back of her mind, that he was there to call on, that he was there in some vague way to protect her, that he was there as a last defence. And if they ever got over their hurt, she had thought, he might be there as a friend.

She lay on the ground for a long time, not crying, just lying there, unwilling and unable to move. Finally, she began looking through her hands at the miniature world in the grass and the moss: tiny gnats and flies and ants, busy having a life, surviving, eating, shitting and dying. There were even flowers — minuscule pink daisies she had never noticed before — hidden under the lank wet grass.

Chapter 18

Louise picked herself up, feeling old and stiff, and considered for a while. Then she drove slowly to Celeste's. When she came through the door, Celeste said crossly, "Marie called. She wants to know if you're coming for supper. She made a big roast, she said, and strawberry pie for desert. Says be sure to be on time. Actually, she invited me and Harold too. I told her I'd leave all the kids home with a frozen pizza but I had to wait and see if you turned up. Where the hell you been anyway?"

"Pruning," said Louise. "Started on the old trees at the farm." She turned away and went to the bathroom to wash, glancing at her face in the mirror: red eyes, shaggy hair with twigs in it, but something more resolved around the chin. Maybe.

Coming back out, she asked, "Hey, do you and Harold own a tent?"

"You don't need a tent," said Celeste, slamming the fridge door. She got out a couple of frozen pizzas and ripped them out of their boxes. "George came by today, looking for you. Said he still had that travel trailer. Harold went to look at it. Says it's pretty nice, actually. It's more than just some dinky travel trailer. It's one of those aluminum jobbies; about twenty-five, thirty feet, Harold says, and all fixed up. I guess George bought it for when he and his wife were going to retire and do some travelling, and then she died of cancer. Anyway, he wants you to have it. Harold and Mark are going to move it out tomorrow after work; they can hook it up to the existing septic, Harold says. All you have to do is get in power and the phone and you're all set."

"Oh my God," said Louise, sitting down.

"You look like hell. When did you sleep last? Go have a shower," said Celeste briskly, "before Harold gets in there and uses up all the hot water. And hurry up, or we're going to be late for dinner."

Dinner was, as always, noisy. Marie, for reasons known only to herself, had invited Mark and Janet and they had left the boys home. Janet had brought a salad and Celeste had mysteriously found time to make bread and buns, which arrived still warm, wrapped in towels. Becky was already there when they arrived, setting the table, chopping vegetables, putting out platters of crackers and cheese and sliced sausage. With relief, Louise saw that none of Becky's other siblings had arrived. She avoided Becky's eyes and slid out of her proffered hug. Becky raised her eyebrows but didn't say anything.

Marie poured out full tumblers of homemade elderberry wine. "You drink up, eh," she said to Louise. "Skinny thing like you needs the vitamins. This is a tonic, you know. Gives you energy. Better than anything you can get from any damn doctor."

Obediently, Louise drank the dark purple-red wine. It slid down her throat in a harmonious chorus of interwoven tastes.

"You ever tap birch trees, eh?" said Marie. For some reason, she seemed determined to talk. "Makes the best wine, clear white. Makes syrup too, but boiling it down takes all day. Who's got the time?"

Finally, they all sat together and ate. The roast was enormous. Harold was invited to carve and he cut thick slabs, round pink steaks lined with yellow fat, for everyone. Janet's salad was out of place — anemic lettuce, laced with shrimp and avocado.

"But it's beautiful, Janet," said Marie. "Just lovely. Too pretty to eat, almost."

Louise and Becky glanced at each other. They knew what Marie thought of avocados. "That foreign junk," she called them. "What's wrong with good homemade coleslaw, cabbage and carrots I grew myself so I know where them came from and no lousy poison sprayed on them?" she had demanded once, long ago, when they had tried to get her to taste an avocado.

"George gave me that old trailer of his," Louise said. "Guess it's time for me to get home and stop living off you folks."

"You come back anytime," said Marie, so Louise knew that she had come to the edge of her welcome.

"Stephen's gonna give me some money," she added cautiously. "So maybe I can afford to start building ..."

"Aw, give it some time yet," rumbled Harold. "What's your hurry? Trailer'll do ya for a while."

"Jeez," said Mark, "talk about living in trailers ... I ever tell you about the time I was staying up at that mining camp up north of the island there? What a weird place ... they had a bunch of trailers and they were all segregated; they had one for the guys, one for the Indians, one for the women cooks and then, way off the side, they had one for the homos."

Everyone stopped eating. "Homos in a mining camp?" someone snorted.

"Yeah," Mark went on. "Bunch of city guys, thought they'd make a few quick bucks ... they didn't last too long. Weird, eh?"

There was another silence.

"Don't make sense," rumbled Becky's dad. "Goddam homos. Just don't make sense, a man with a man. Shit." He shook his head. Someone snickered. "Don't make sense," he muttered again. Then the talk changed just as suddenly to the flammability of trailers and how fast they might burn, and how hot aluminum burned once it was actually on fire, and how they used to make trailers out of magnesium, like airplanes, so they burned like white hot bombs.

But Louise had ceased to listen. She sat very quietly, eating her dinner. She wondered how soon she could decently excuse herself and get away. To save herself, she thought of the cool thick mud in the swamp, the darkness under the trees and how she could go away and hide there. She thought of the mountains shimmering blue fire in the moonlight, and how, if she wanted, she could wander free there, how she could take herself away into the mountains and not be seen again. The room was too hot and there seemed to be an endless amount of food to get through. She ate as fast as she could, while the conversation swooped and bellowed around her like a high wind.

Everyone finally seemed to be finished. Louise got up and began carrying the empty bowls and dirty plates into the kitchen, stacking them by the dishwasher. Marie sliced cake and opened jars of canned peaches and pears. She brought out pies from the fridge and filled a plate with cookies.

After the dishes were done, Louise went outside and sat on the steps. The river was roaring inside its banks, rising now in its annual, brown, freezing-cold flood. She sat there for a long time, listening to the river, listening to the noise inside and the noise outside, on the edge of the steps, unable to make herself move.

Louise didn't say anything at all when Becky came outside. She didn't go back in and say goodnight. Instead, she and Becky walked together across the yard to the trailer. Inside, she went to the bathroom, got into a nightgown and crawled quickly into bed. Becky looked at her once or twice but didn't say anything.

"Want some tea?" Becky asked finally. "I noticed you didn't have anything after dinner."

Louise shook her head.

"How was your day?" Becky asked. "You figure out what you're going to do?"

"I'm leaving," Louise said. "I'm going away. Somewhere."

Becky didn't answer. She filled a kettle with water and put it on the gas stove.

Then she sat down on the bed, facing Louise.

"You talk to Stephen?" she asked.

Louise nodded. "He knew about the drugs," she said. "It was some guy he knew, Sam Edwards, that fat drunken slob. Stephen's his lawyer. Stephen knew all along. He said he'd give me the money I want. He said there wasn't any case and just to forget the whole thing."

"He say who burned your house?"

"No," she said bitterly. "That didn't even seem important, in the scheme of things. What's an old house matter to anyone? Now I've got the money to build a new one, so who cares?" She paused, hesitating. Then she said, "Becky, did you know any of this?"

Becky sighed. "I sort of guessed," she said. "You hear things. I was trying to find out for sure before I said anything. I didn't want you to get too involved. From what I've heard, these guys are mean and they play dirty. But tell you the truth, I don't know about your house. Can't quite figure it. No percentage in it. But then there's the phone calls." She stopped, frowned, walked across the floor, came back and sat down.

"They know better than to mess with me, I guess, but the problem is you're too easy a target."

"What do you mean? Why wouldn't they mess with you? What's the difference?"

"Because."

"Because you deal too."

"No, I don't deal. I smoke a little. I've grown the odd patch; I get around. I just know too much. And I have friends who know too much."

"But I'm too stupid to know anything. So I get left out here in the dark, flailing around and looking like an idiot and getting my house burnt down or burning my own goddamn house down, what's the difference."

"You're not stupid, Lou."

"No? So why didn't you tell me? Why didn't you trust me with what you know. How come we didn't share what we knew? Were you afraid I'd find out too much? If the cops get involved, then everyone has to run for the hills. I don't give a shit who smokes or grows or deals. But Celia got hurt. I got hurt. And you owed us. You owed me! So what kind of friendship is this?"

"It's not that simple."

"Oh, fuck off. It is that simple. We're friends or we're not friends. Actually, I don't even know what the word means anymore. Stephen and I were going to be friends. Susan told me she was my friend. Your family are my friends but they hate homos. So, who do I talk to? Who can I trust? I don't even know what's up or down anymore. I don't understand anything. That's why I've got to go. I've got to figure things out and the only way to do that, as I see it, is to find out the rules, find out how things really work. I don't even know where to start looking but I'll find out. Stupid old Lou. Everybody's friend. Well, fuck it. From now on, I'm going to look after myself, just like everyone else is doing."

Becky didn't say anything. She got up and made the tea, waited while it steeped, then poured it into delicate, gold-edged cups and brought it back to the bed.

"I'm sorry, Lou," she said. "I'm sorry you feel this way. But I am your friend, no matter what you think. And Stephen's just an arrogant jerk who doesn't know his ass from a hole in the ground and you're well rid of him. And so — my Dad's an ignorant old Mick. But he didn't mean anything. He wouldn't care about you and Susan, even if he knew. My Dad invented the word clannish. You're part of his clan, part of this family, part of this community. It's outsiders he really hates. You'd have to practically murder someone before he would stop defending you. He's still your friend. And besides, why should it matter that much to you?"

"It just does. How am I supposed to look your parents in the eye? I feel so shitty. There are always going to be people saying things like your Dad did tonight. There's nothing I can do about it. I'm always going to hear things, everyone trashes people like me. No one thinks

about it. It's just something they do. And it hurts, you know. So I keep
wondering, how the hell am I supposed to go on living here?"

"Because you're the same damn person you've always been, that
we've always known. You've been coming over here and hanging out
with my family for a long time. So what's changed? There's nothing
new, nothing you didn't know before."

"No … it's not the same … I'm not the same." She paused. "No,
that's not it. I feel the same … but I'm not. I have to go away, Beck. I
just don't see any option. How can I live here anymore? I just don't see
it. I don't know what to do … don't want to leave, don't want to stay."

"So go away. Jeezus. What difference does it make? You can come
and go all you want. We'll still be here, and the land and the river and
the mountains, and your new trailer, and your friend. Go do whatever
you need to. It's okay. It's okay, Lou. You can go. You can come back.
You're free as a breeze. It'll be fine. What's your damn problem? God,
you make such a huge deal out of things. It'll all work out."

Louise stared at Becky's face.

"You don't get it, do you? You don't know what I'm talking about."
She put her head on her knees. Her throat closed. "I didn't do anything
wrong. But I feel like shit. I feel embarrassed. I feel like apologizing for
walking down the street in town. I feel like everyone would hate me if
they knew what I was and I don't know why." The words choked out,
one at a time. Becky said nothing, watched her, listening.

"Jeezus!" Louise exploded. "I didn't ask for any of this. I loved my
family, I love your goddamn family, I love you and Celeste and Harold
and Celia, and I loved Susan. What's the difference?"

"There isn't any," Becky said softly.

"Then why do I feel so lousy about it? Why does it feel like I
committed a crime that's too terrible to even talk about?"

"I don't know," said Becky. "Maybe you're making too much out
of it. People don't care that much. I think you worry about it too much.
People forget quickly. It'll be okay."

"Maybe," Louise said, turning her face away. "Maybe it will be
okay. I don't know. You're right. It doesn't matter. Forget it."

She turned away to sleep, turned away from Becky's offered hug.
She gathered blankets around her, gathering in the pieces of the day,
desperately hunting sleep like a remedy. But it was a long time coming.

She listened instead to Becky's breathing, a dog barking somewhere
across the river, the river slowly grinding gravel into sand. She took thin
hanks of her hair and twisted and twisted the ends into fragments.

Chapter 19

The trailer was, surprisingly enough, just what Louise needed. It was small — a twenty-five-foot-long steel box, a little smaller than the trailer Becky lived in. Although it had once been meant only for travel, George had built drawers and stuck shelves into odd nooks and crannies so that there was an abundance of storage. It had bright yellow-and-white checked wallpaper beside the sink, and just enough room to stand and cook at the propane stove. The tiny propane furnace under the counter meant it was always warm. It took Louise a while to get used to waking in the morning to a warm space.

Harold and Mark had positioned the trailer on a small knoll just to the north of the remains of the burnt house; the window in the living room looked out over the pasture and down to the river, and the trailer faced south towards the border. When Louise had first walked in with Mark and Harold, she had sunk to her knees on the shaggy green carpet in front of the view. The sill of the window was only a foot above the floor. She saw herself there in the evenings, carving, a teapot beside her; she imagined many cushions, silence and a place in which to be, again, at home.

Because she had nothing to move in with, the trailer remained relatively spacious and clean and new, even after she had spent the night there, even after she had made tea at the new stove and washed cups in the sink. Hot and cold water ran like a miracle. The bed was built in; there was little to buy after she had gone to town and bought some cast iron pots and pans and a bright Indian patterned blanket. Besides, she had enough donations to furnish several trailers. She left most of that stuff stacked in boxes, taking up room in Celeste's garage. She didn't know what else to do with it.

The money from Stephen was in the bank; it had come in the mail, in a cheque. She had looked at it, gone to the bank, said nothing to the teller, endorsed it and handed it over. The woman had looked at the name, deposited it and handed her back a deposit slip. Louise thought she should spend some of it — buy herself a present — but the thought of actually going and buying something with the money made her feel sick. She phoned George, thanked him, and offered, hesitantly, to pay for the trailer.

"Don't say nothing more about it," he growled. "Just keep coming in to work. Them trees ain't going to wait forever now, are they? And them other guys aren't worth the powder to blow them to hell. All they're good for is heading for the bar after work."

So she didn't know what to do with the money. She supposed she should investigate some kind of investment; she should be responsible with it. She thought again of things she could get — a sewing machine for Celeste, presents for everyone. She didn't know what to get. Maybe something for Celia. What would Celia like? She didn't know anymore.

Stephen had accused her of not understanding money, of being irresponsible with it, of not caring about it. But, come to think of it, he had said that only after she had moved out and didn't have any. Now, she thought about trying to do something — she had heard vague things about investment funds and mutual funds and interest rates. But she couldn't bring herself to walk into the bank and ask; not yet, anyway. So the money rested undisturbed.

She hadn't called Becky and Becky hadn't come by. Marie had called to invite her to dinner, but she had made an excuse. Then she heard that Becky was away — gone treeplanting, gone without saying goodbye. "So much for that friendship," she said out loud to the trailer walls. So much for friendship, period.

Celeste was busy and distant. Louise had told her about her confrontation with Stephen, about Sam Edwards and his involvement in drug smuggling. To her surprise, Celeste had seemed offended, as if her friendship with Louise was somehow responsible for this connection. Since then, despite Louise's open cynicism, Celeste had enrolled Celia in a youth group at one of the churches. One of the requirements was that Celeste and Harold go to the parents' Bible study. Celeste was overly enthusiastic about the changes she tought Celia was making. She tried to explain how terrific it all was to Louise, who said nothing, kept a straight face, and nodded appropriately. But Celeste was suspicious. She pushed. Finally, Louise said she thought the whole thing was a crock.

"Thanks a lot," said Celeste. "You're the one who demanded I do something. You're the one who seems to think this whole mess is my fault because I haven't done all the right things you figured out all by yourself that I ought to do. Well, now I've done something and all you can do is criticize."

Louise never argued with Celeste when she had an idea of this kind in her head. It was like arguing with a logging truck on a steep road. She didn't argue now. She changed the subject. But when she phoned, Celeste's voice was always very bright and cheerful. Louise wanted to strangle her. She wondered how far they could stretch the friendship and still keep it intact. Maybe now that she had some money, she thought, the strange cruel winds of fate were blowing away everything else she cared about.

Soon after the trailer was installed, Louise went back to working for George. She'd tried again to thank him for the trailer, but he'd merely grunted and walked away from her. She'd also written for catalogues from several universities, and in the evenings she leafed through them, reading the descriptions of the courses, the possibilities for different degrees and different kinds of training. She found the whole thing confusing but exhilarating to think about. At night, before she went to sleep, she thought of the money sitting safely in the bank and the things she might do with it. She sent away for several mail-order catalogues and read through them, thinking to herself, *I can afford this. I can afford this.* She read through catalogues for furniture, clothes and tools. She looked at ads for new cars. She remembered going shopping with her mother and the light in her mother's eyes when Louise would buy thick heavy towels, and sheets with expansive, violent flowers patterned across them. She made out an order for herself from one catalogue that sold hiking boots and tents and sleeping bags. But she never mailed it. Finally she stacked the catalogues in a corner bookshelf.

She did buy books. One day, she took some of Stephen's money from the bank and went on a drunken book binge. She drove, by herself, to the next town and went to the bookstore and bought whole shopping bags of books. She bought poetry by writers she had never heard of and novels that sounded promising and books on the environment and women and history and farming and gardening. She brought them home and stacked them on the floor. At night, she sat on the floor by the heater and read bits at random from all of them. Sometimes, in the middle of her reading, she'd think about Stephen again and the thoughts went around in her head, wearing a bitter groove. Over and over, she thought about what she should have said, about things that still needed saying. Sometimes, she pulled the phone towards her and picked up the receiver. Then she put it down again.

"I hate you," she would say, very softly. "I hate you. I hate you, I hate you." But she didn't convince herself. Then she would go back to her reading.

She bought seeds and planted a garden; she mowed the lawn; she cleaned up the burnt house site, trucking away to the dump the twisted remains of her stove, her bed, crumbled and unrecognizable bits and pieces of the house. She worked at George's every day until dark, then came home and read until her eyes drooped. She still lay awake in bed every night, staring at the wall where she had taped a poster of a wild black stallion.

One night, she went out to the woodpile and, after some searching, found the piece of cedar she had laid aside before her house had burned down. She stared at it for a while and then began, very hesitantly, to chip away and slice off bits of pieces of the wood. In the morning, it was sitting on the small arborite kitchen table, waiting for her. During the day, while she clipped and sawed her way through one tree after another, her hands would remember the smooth, sliding feel of the knife, the soapy slipperiness of wood. Sometimes, though, the carving failed and, instead, she would get dressed again, drive the long drive to town, go to the 7-11, read through the magazines, make trival conversation about the weather with the bored and sleepy clerk, and come home.

She was absurdly surprised and pleased one Sunday morning when Celeste phoned to ask if Celia could come over to go riding. When they drove in the yard, Louise made coffee and put out the plate of cookies she had just made, and they talked over the local gossip while the sun streamed in the window onto the green and yellow wallpaper. Then Celeste drove away and she and Celia caught and saddled the horses. They rode and slid down the gravel trail to the river and took a shortcut through an old hayfield. There, they found some hay bales left over from winter and made the horses jump over them, then raced at a dead gallop around the whole wide field, laughing their exuberance while the horses flicked their tails and snorted, and geese flew ahead of them across the yellow stubble.

But when Louise next went to Celeste's for coffee, Celeste was still too bright and too cheerful about everything. They both still talked around the edges of all the subjects they couldn't discuss.

When Louise was too tired for carving or driving she lay awake, listening for the crunch of tires on the gravel road up the hill from the trailer. She practised noticing who was driving by and she kept track of license plates. She told herself she was being ridiculous, making a melodrama of something which was finished and done with, and which, probably, she would never quite understand.

Then one night, the calls started again. The phone rang and rang; each time she picked it up, she heard the wires singing weirdly into emptiness. She heard her heart beating softly in the silence of the trailer — it was so silent that she could hear the electric clock radio clucking to itself. She thought she should get a dog; but then, if she left to go to school, she would have to give it away again. After that, as she drove home from work she watched the shape the hill made against the mountains, watched for the first flash of sunlight gleaming off aluminum; but the trailer was always there, locked and quiet, waiting.

When Celeste phoned to ask her one day what she was doing with herself, and why hadn't she been over, she surprised them both by snapping fiercely, "I'm staying alive." Even to her own ears, it sounded foolishly dramatic.

But Celeste sighed deeply into the phone. "Yeah, what a shitty year," she said. "What we ever did to deserve this, I'll never figure out. If God is so goddamn all knowing, I wish he'd figure this latest piece of shit out. Save us a lot of trouble. Come over here. I have something to show you."

When Louise arrived at Celeste's, Celeste demanded immediately, "Here. Look at this." She grabbed a piece of paper and slammed it on the table. Louise picked it up and read it. It took her a while to figure it out. It was a letter from the sawmill where Harold delivered logs, warning him that his performance had been "unsatisfactory," and, due to possible layoffs in the future, he was being placed on some kind of "list."

"I don't get it," Louise said in disbelief. "Harold? Harold's the best driver they've got, works his ass off, never complains. Besides, he doesn't work for them. He's his own boss. What is this crap?"

"Word we've got is that your friend, Sam Edwards, is working at the mill as some kind of PR hack."

"What? The mill? But ... I thought he left town."

"Well, guess he came back."

"So, this is still related to Celia."

"Looks that way."

"Oh my God, Celeste. What the hell have we smacked into here?"

"I don't know. I can't figure it out. What good does it do anyone to pick on Harold? What do they want us to do, leave the goddamn country?"

"I don't know. None of this makes sense. It hasn't made sense from the beginning. Why Celia? Why me? Why burn my house down? Why Harold, for God's sake?"

"I don't know, Lou. Did you hear about that hitchhiker disappearing? I guess the cops have been looking for him. He was camping or something. No one seems to know who he was, and I'm sure it has nothing to do with us. But I'm getting scared. This used to be such a quiet peaceful kind of place. I don't know what's going on. I don't know anything about this kind of stuff. Harold and I are just plain people, trying to get by and do the best we can. What happened to Celia was shitty, but we're managing. She's coming around. She even let me take her shopping the other day and buy her something more than torn blue jeans. I don't need any more crap. I can't take any more crap." Celeste's voice rose. She put her hands on the table to steady herself. Louise stared at her. Celeste was shaking all over. *Like a leaf*, Louise thought. *So that's what it looks like.* Celeste did look like a poplar leaf in a high wind.

"I'm scared too, Cel," Louise said slowly. "But I'm not sure fear's going to help us much. We're going to have to be smarter. We're going to have to figure this out. We're going to have to fight back somehow. We can't just take this. It's not fair."

She told Celeste about the phone ringing. They sat together through the afternoon, reluctant to break the fragile shell of safety around their togetherness. Celeste mentioned that she was probably going to quit the Bible study. "Hell, maybe I'm a Christian and maybe I'm not. Maybe I'm just not the right type of person but I sure don't have it all figured out like that uptight prissy bunch. Actually, they weren't even friendly. They just wanted us there like trophies on their shelves."

Rain slanted against the windows. It had been a slow, cold, late spring. After showing a brief warm promise in February, spring had come in fits and starts. Celeste and Louise commiserated with each other on their efforts to get a garden started. Finally, reluctantly, Louise drove home; she worked outside until dark, weeding the wet flower beds in the cold gloomy evening. Even then, she was reluctant to go inside and face the necessity of closing the curtains and turning on the lights against the darkness outside.

At midnight, she went to bed and lay staring at the black sky outside the window. Her inability to sleep made her furious. She was tired. She had to work tomorrow. It was Stephen's fault, all of it. Or hers. Or the town's, or God's — depending on how you looked at it.

Now it had all come back again. She couldn't live like this, in limbo. The words fit. They chimed in her head: "In limbo." The next morning, it was still raining. She phoned George, who said, gruffly, of course she shouldn't come in, was she crazy?

She phoned her lawyer and drove the long, tedious two hour drive to his office the next town. Before her appointment, she bought lunch and went to the bookstore and bought another bag of books. When she came out, it had stopped raining and the faint sun on the sidewalk evoked misty steam tendrils, which curled gently around her legs.

The lawyer listened to her story. Every once in a while, he doodled a note on a piece of paper, frowning. When she finished, he sat and stared at her. "Well, you're right," he said. "You've got a problem. But I don't know what you think I can do about it."

"I don't know what you can do about it either," Louise said. "I just needed to know if it sounded crazy … if I sounded crazy. I needed to say it out loud to someone."

"No, you don't sound crazy," the lawyer said. "I just don't know how I can help. I'd like to. I've heard some things myself. But I'm a lawyer, not an investigator. Now you've got money, why do you stick around? You know, I don't understand, myself, what keeps some people in these places. They don't have to stay. My God, how do they stand it — no movies, theatre, restaurants. No energy. This place is such a vacuum. Nothing comes in or goes out. No new ideas. No culture." He shuddered delicately, and waited for her response. Louise realized, with some surprise, that he was only talking about himself, not her — that, in fact, he had lost interest in her.

"My wife and I made an agreement that we would try it here for five years," he finally continued. "Then we're getting out and going back to the coast. We thought it would be better to bring children up here but, my God, the school system! And there's just as much crime and what-not as there is in the city. At least there you can protect them by sending them to good schools." He sniffed.

She nodded, trying, with some difficulty, to look polite and interested. But he was finished.

"Well, good luck," he said, standing up but not smiling. He was obviously glad to see her go. "I'm sorry I couldn't help you with this. Let me know if there's anything else I can do."

When she got home again, it was dark. She didn't turn the lights on in the trailer, even though she was hungry and cold. She paced in the dark, thinking. Then she phoned Celeste.

"I have to talk to Celia," she said. "It's important. Don't ask. I'll tell you about it later."

"Celia," she said, when Celia came to the phone. "You *have* to tell me the name of that kid, the one who gave you the drugs. I know you don't want to, but you have to. I have to know. Don't ask any questions. Just tell me."

Celia was silent. Finally, she said, in a tiny girl's voice, "Is this about Dad?"

" Yes," Louise said flatly. "It is."

"His name is Brian," Celia said. "Brian Hepher."

In the dark, Louise nodded. Then she turned on the light, looked up his name and dialed.

The voice that answered the phone was that of a boy, young and uncertain.

"Brian Hepher?" Louise asked.

"Yeah, yeah, that's me, okay, you got me," said the voice cheerfully, althought it was blurry around the edges. Maybe there was some party she had interrupted. "So, what do you want, sell me something?" he giggled. Louise could hear other voices in the background. The boy yelled something away from the phone which she couldn't catch. There was a crash and a lot of laughter.

"I'm a friend of Celia's," she said. "I need to talk to you."

The silence on the other end stretched into her fear — hooked into it like claws.

"I don't think I'm, like, I mean, I don't want to talk to you," he said.

"Look," said Louise. "Celia's in trouble and you let her take the rap. Now you owe her; you owe her family. I don't want to do anything. I just want to talk to you. Please. I'm not going to get you into trouble. I'm not trying to get anyone into trouble. I'm just trying to understand what's been going on. I need to understand."

"It was just stupid," the boy said, lowering his voice until he was almost whispering into the phone. "Just kid's stuff. Nothing was supposed to happen."

"But it did," she said. "And Celia got hurt and so did her parents. They're good people. They didn't deserve this. I'm sure you didn't expect anything to go wrong. But it did. I'm sure that you're a good person too. Celia seems to think a lot of you."

"She does?" the voice was startled.

"Yeah, she does," Louise snapped back. "Why do you think she didn't say anything? She's been protecting you through this whole mess."

"Oh," he said. She waited. His voice, when he spoke, sprayed need and desperation, although it was covered with a jaunty attempt to sound okay. "Hey, where are you?" he asked. "I guess it would be okay. Maybe I could tell you something, explain it a bit and you could talk to Celia for me. She won't even look at me anymore."

"I'm out in the boonies," she said. "But I'll come into town."

"No, somebody might see something, figure out that I talked to you. Do you know the turnout by the river?"

"Sure," she said. "Okay ... I'll be there in about, oh, twenty minutes."

Louise changed into black clothes, and then, feeling ridiculous, pulled a black hat over her hair. Driving badly, skidding on the gravel, she made it to the river road and down as far as the turnout. She went past it, not seeing a car, then pulled over to the side of the road, left the truck and walked back.

When the boy showed up, he was alone. He turned off his car headlights and waited. She went back and got the truck, and drove in behind him a few minutes later.

He was younger looking than she had expected; somehow, his voice had sounded older, warier — too old and wary for sixteen. He was good looking, with black hair and dark blue eyes, but his face was still round and undefined; his voice when he said hello cracked with uncertainty.

"Look," he said, without any preamble. "Celia got a rotten deal. That was shitty ... what they did. It wasn't her fault. They could have just let her go. But the pigs, man, they had to have someone to lay it on."

"Yeah, well, you played a role too," Louise snapped, "and it's not your family getting pushed around. Not your house that burnt. You still look pretty healthy."

"They did that? Burnt your house?" His voice squeaked. Louise almost laughed, but when she spoke her voice rasped like a saw. She felt it inside, her own voice tearing at her throat muscles. "And threatened Celia's father with losing his job."

"Man, that's so shitty."

He was pacing in front of her, shaking his head, saying, "man, man," over and over, wincing as if he had been struck and was trying to recover from the blow.

She wondered how much was acting and how much was bewilderment. Sixteen was young to be dealing with this kind of trouble. Most days she couldn't believe it herself; she still woke up each morning with a sickening sense of fearful confusion, as though the world had gone unexpectedly and absurdly out of kilter and was refusing to right itself. But she'd been stupid and bewildered so long that the sickness was also slowly transforming, like a huge and sleepy beast, and coming awake — into anger. It didn't even matter who or what she was angry at. But she hadn't realized, until she heard her voice come ripping out of her throat, how her anger had metamorphosed.

Maybe being as klutzy and ignorant as she manifestly had been was some kind of advantage at the moment. After all, knowing nothing at all, she was now ready to forge some kind of direction for herself. She had spent long enough just giving up, curled into a heap like the snakes she and Mark had tormented as kids — out in the hayfield, startling them into jumping like gazelles. If the snake was in the open, and they could get ahead of it, they had run frantic gleeful circles around it, thumping their feet hard on the ground to make it slow, stop, and test the air with a flickering agile tongue, testing for the vibrations, the thunderous resonant crashing of bare feet on stubble, around and around, the snake coiling in desperate keenness, looking for a direction and finding only noise and more noise. If they had kept it up — kept up the noise — the snake eventually curled into itself, despondent, trapped, with no way out. It rested until, giving up, they let it go. Or sometimes the snake found a hole in the bordering territory of noise and slipped through, greased itself through the grass stalks and disappeared. It had been a game, nothing more, to them.

"It was just, kind of like, you know, a game. Hell, it's easy to get stuff through the border. Everyone does it — booze, cigarettes, you name it. Drugs are just a part of it."

Louise nodded. Even she'd played that game, once, driving through the back roads with her friends and several open cases of American beer. She hadn't done it again. That was more Mark's game.

"Then it started to get weird. Like, serious. Very serious. I kind of got scared and quit. That night when Celia was with us was the last night we did anything."

"I was sort of depressed for a while," he added, very softly. "I tried to hurt myself." He held out his wrists with a brief grin, somewhere between proud and perplexed, as if he still had no idea how he felt about the possibility of his own death. The scars crossed and re-crossed his arms like threads, not just his wrists, but all up and down the fleshy part of his forearms. Louise stared.

"I tried going to a counsellor for a while. Actually, he helped me a lot. I don't feel so lousy about everything now. He's like, into meditation and stuff. You know? Stuff like that is really cool."

"Great," she thought. "That should solve all your problems."

"And that's it?" she said out loud. She tried to keep her voice even, not desperate, not, for God's sake, pleading with this sad baby. "You're not going to do anything more? You could turn these guys in. The cops would protect you. It would make a huge difference to this town. I mean, you can sense that there's something wrong. People ..."

"No," he said. "I can't do that."

"But why not?"

"I just can't. Listen, I'd better go. I've got stuff to do."

He stood there with his awkward hands hanging at his sides, a too-large boy, a half-grown man.

Louise knew she had to say something more. "We just want to be left alone," she said. "That's it. Can you understand that? We're just barely surviving as it is; we're not any part of this. We just want to be left alone." But the boy was already moving away. He was the wrong person to say this to.

Louise watched him go. He spun the truck on the gravel — whether from nervousness or to show off, she didn't know. What a male thing to do, she thought — just to show her ... something. That he wasn't just a boy, too young and too powerless to take care of his friends or himself.

The lights and the hum from the motor disappeared down the road, and were replaced by the low grumble of water in the river. A few birds were still awake — geese far away, gossiping with each other. Lucky geese, she thought, with only their own problems to deal with, their own assurance in the night, a lifetime of knowledge and security, interrupted occasionally by guns and noise and slaughter.

Abruptly, she felt such disgust for herself and her kind that she wanted to throw up. This wide sandy area by the bend in the river was

littered with debris, broken glass, a few old tires, a dusty car wreck
towed in under the cottonwood trees and disowned. There were heaps
of lumpy charcoal left over from old fires; tree branches stupidly torn
from trees and too green to be of any use as fuel; coke and pepsi bottles;
torn chip bags. She found a torn plastic garbage bag and wandered
around, picking up garbage. When the bag wouldn't hold anymore, she
threw it in the back of her truck and climbed in the cab and the ugly
image of the sad boy with his scarred wrists followed her inside. She
supposed he must be about half crazy. Perhaps his willingness to talk
with her had been a bid for attention, or a way of trying to convince
Celia and himself of his good intentions, of both his guilt and his
innocence. But why were there scars all over his arms? The delicate
razor edge slicing through flesh was an antidote to what — the rest of
his life?

Finally, she started the truck and, slowly and sedately, drove home.
Spinning her tires on the gravel gave her no satisfaction anymore. She
felt very tired. Maybe she would have a bath and watch television and
not read at all — just go to bed and not think about anything.

She felt like she had lost some battle she hadn't realized she was
fighting — one she hadn't noticed, one that had been going on all
around her while she was struggling to prune trees and keep her truck
running. Or, maybe, they were the same battle. She couldn't tell
anymore.

Chapter 20

Becky called: Treeplanting season was over. She was cheerful on the phone; glad to be home, she said, glad to see everyone. Louise was startled to hear from her, tried to remember that she was still mad, tried to stay gloomy and stand-offish, but, in truth, she was glad to hear from Becky. Nothing like that ever worked with Becky anyway.

"Come over," Becky said, her usual pushy self. "Let's go down to the river, drink a few beers, go canoeing. You can tell me all the news and everything you've been doing with yourself."

After Louise hung up the phone she was annoyed with both herself and Becky. Once more, she was acting like a puppet. She should have said no, or argued, or suggested something different. She should have let Becky know that she was still angry. She should have asserted herself. "You're so damn passive," she scolded herself. It was just another tiny piece of the helplessness she had felt all summer and was still feeling. Everything around her confirmed the helplessness: Every time she went into the town, she always saw the same people doing the same things. Nothing would ever change again, she thought. She had set her life in a pattern now and she was stuck with it. Although, this evening, if she admitted the truth to herself, she really wanted to see Becky. Having someone with whom to play at the river, someone with whom to swim and eat and goof around in the canoe, sounded like a relief from another long evening in the trailer with her books or television or her own smoldering, futile anger.

She hardly ever went to Celeste's these days. Celeste was never much fun, reflected Louise. She was a friend — someone to be with —

but she wasn't much good at thinking up things to do, especially in the summer when the heat made her cranky and the kids drove her crazy hanging around inside the house with the TV on. Sometimes, she made them turn it off and drove them outside, a strategy which never lasted long because then Celeste herself would go outside to work in the garden and the kids would drift immediately back into the house, where they fed themselves on bowls of cheap noodle soup and crackers and potato chips and frozen French fries, all of it heated in the microwave. The dishes piled in the sink until Celeste snarled at someone to wash them or did them herself.

"Well, why do you buy that crap then?" Louise said, whenever Celeste complained about the kids' eating habits, but Celeste only shrugged.

"At least they eat it," she said. Celeste also made a huge dinner every night, with giant bowls of salad and mashed potatoes and slabs of roast beef, or chicken or pork chops, so Louise supposed the kids must be getting some nutrition. But, in the summers, the house was grubby with heat and too many bodies and the smell of food drying on the dishes. No wonder Celeste fled to the garden, where she wandered around picking flowers and pulling weeds which grew back immediately since only pulled their tops off. Sometimes, in a state of complete frenzy at how messy things had become, she mowed the grass, steering the ancient lawn mower around the piles of old engines and truck parts and rusting oil barrels and stray bits of metal left over from Harold working whatever mysterious alchemy he worked in the deep, black intricacies of his many machines. Often she and Harold would make plans for the yard, but Harold had his work and Celeste had the kids. Plans to change things, fix things, improve things, took time and energy and money. Plans could always wait, and they did.

Louise made an effort, these days, to talk to Harold. She was glad for his awkward kindness. Somehow, when her house had burned down and she had seen his face, she had seen the Harold who was also her friend. He tried to respond. He would show her around his machines and talk to her as if she knew something of what he was doing. She stood it politely for a respectable length of time before fleeing, to their great mutual relief, into the house to talk to Celeste.

The evening light was brilliant with gold and dust as Louise drove to the river. Becky was there waiting, with the sleek red canoe that she had bought years ago off some city people who had moved to the country to live close to the land. They had lasted six months and fled.

"C'mon," she said, impatiently. "God, you're slow. I've been wait-ing for hours. Let's paddle down to the point, where there'll be a wind and no bugs and we can make a fire and dinner."

"I brought some cheese and bagels," Louise said tentatively.

"Yeah, well I packed up dinner with all the leftovers from Ma's, so don't worry about food," Becky grinned. Silently, Louise climbed in the canoe. Why was Becky always three steps ahead of her? Whatever Louise did, Becky did it faster and better. She hadn't mentioned food on the phone. Louise felt petty and mean and discontented. Everything these days added to her discontentment.

They let the canoe slide lazily over the current, past the few rocks, under the cottonwood trees dropping sticks and bits of fluff on the clear green water. Louise looked down through the water to the bottom, which was mostly mud alternating with rocky sand bars. Automatically, she looked for fish, a habit she had developed when she was a kid, fishing with her Dad.

"So, tell me, what did you finally do about old Steve, and Celia and the local drug cartel?" Becky said cheerfully.

"Nothing is what I did," said Louise, still gloomy and angry and wishing Becky would quit being so cheerful. "Nothing at all. What the hell could I do? I found out everything I could. But they got away with it. The vicious bastards, whoever they are, burned my house, threat-ened Harold, turned Celia into a juvie. I talked to my lawyer. He wasn't even very interested. I thought and thought about it but I felt like no matter where I turned, I was blocked. And I was scared actually. You're right. These guys are rough. They must be to do what they did. So finally I met up with Celia's friend, this weird boy named Brian Hepher, got knife scars all over his arms. And I told him to tell whoever they are to leave us alone. And they have, I guess. Anyway, it's been a quiet summer. Just been going to work every day — keeps George happy, anyway — working and reading and reading. And carving," she added suddenly.

"You carve?" said Becky. "Since when? Carve what? You never told me. Hey, I wanta see, are they at your house?"

"It's nothing," muttered Louise. "Forget it. It's nothing."

But Becky was delighted. "You little sneak," she said. "Sitting around being a carver and never telling me a thing. So, what have you made?"

"Well, a horse," Louise said, staring at the water. Actually, she was proud of the horse. It was the first thing she'd carved that really looked like something. It had taken her the last couple of months; it was the first thing she'd completely finished, right down to sanding and polishing and varnishing. Then she had put it on the polished surface of the tiny desk in her tiny bedroom where she could look at it in the mornings where the sun came in the window and turned it into a bright shining signal.

"And a deer," she added. The deer hadn't turned out so well. The face was too delicate to carve properly, and she'd sliced off half its nose. You could still tell it was a deer, but she'd hidden that one.

"My," said Becky. "Well, I'm going to have a look when I come over. So what else have you been doing? Besides fuming at stupid assholes and carving."

"Gardening. Cleaning up the mess from the fire. Keeping to myself." She felt suddenly shy and a bit desperate. She wanted to tell Becky how ridiculous her summer had been, how long the evenings in the trailer were, with only with the books and maybe a walk or a ride. She wanted to tell her how, sometimes, she sat outside talking to the horses. She wanted to say that she sat beside the phone and made up long angry conversations with Stephen; she wanted to talk about the despair she felt when she looked ahead and tried to decide what to do with her life.

"I'm sorry I didn't see you before I left," Becky said. "I got the call and I had to leave the same day. I came by your trailer but you were out. Didn't even have time to leave you a note. I was with a whole car of people."

"Oh," said Louise. "Yeah, sorry I missed you."

"Yeah, I'm sorry too."

They were silent together.

"Look," said Becky suddenly. "Stephen's going to get his, you know. Those kinds of guys always do. They overreach themselves, or they do something stupid or they end up with cancer and ulcers and varicose veins. Don't worry about him. He's not worth it. The whole thing is cosmic anyway. It all balances out, eh?" she grinned.

"Yes, but I don't want to wait for any goddamn cosmic balancing out," Louise said gloomily. "I want to do something about it now. I wanted to be the big hero, I guess. Like I hadn't screwed up everything else in my life … I thought I could maybe play maverick cop, just like in the movies … only, of course, it didn't work and I couldn't make it work. It's been killing me all summer, what a loser I am. This was the final straw."

When she said it, Louise felt the whole weight of it again: the sorrow over her house, the worry over Celia and Celeste, her love for them, the old pain from Susan and, under that, the old pain from Stephen. She leaned over the side of the canoe, trailing her paddle in the water, looking down again through its shimmering green depths.

"You weren't the cause of any of that shit, you know," Becky said and her voice was very quiet. "Stephen is a crook and Celia's a kid and Celeste, much as I love her, is a dim bulb at times, and you ... all you tried to do was help ... all you ever tried to do is what's right, be a good daughter, marry a normal man and then you fell in love and you went with that and it didn't work out but you had the guts to try. And now, when your friend phones you and hollers for help on something that isn't even your problem, you worry and try to move mountains and when they won't fucking move, you blame yourself. Have you ever thought of blaming the goddamn mountain for being in your way? Or maybe just going around it? Or ignoring it?"

"I failed," said Louise, stubbornly. "Again."

"Yeah, and you love it. Because if you quit being a failure, you'd have to look around and realize that you're just a nice normal fine person and a few people love and care about you. And wouldn't that just blow your little trip all to hell."

There was silence in the canoe. Then Becky laughed. She splashed water at Louise with the paddle. "Jeezus god allmuddy! Get real, McDonald," she yelled, "or I'll just dump you in the river to see if you can swim."

Louise looked at Becky. She was still laughing. Louise didn't feel much like laughing. "It's true," she said. "I failed. I couldn't finish it. Like all the other things in my life I didn't finish."

"This is not quite on the same level, kid. This is something you didn't make any decisions about. The whole thing was forced on you."

"I know that," Louise's voice was desperate. "And somehow that's all part of it — that it doesn't make any sense, that it's just this stupid thing that happened. That I couldn't, that I can't, do anything about. It's driving me crazy."

Becky was silent for a while. They let the canoe drift with the current in idle lazy circles. The brilliant red sides shone in the water. The sun was already below the mountains and the evening light lingered on, tinging everything with gold and lavendar.

"So," Becky said matter-of-factly. "What else could you have done? What could we do now? It sounds like you did what you could ... short of shooting that creep, Sam." She paused, then added, "You know, all we really need to do, if we could, is get some of these kids to talk. If we promised them it would all be anonymous, y'know, did some kind of investigation, got it into the right hands ... all we really need is some good evidence. Then somebody would have to at least have an investigation, shake things up a bit."

"Yeah?" said Louise, trying not to let hope light up her voice.

"Yeah," said Becky. She frowned, thinking out loud. "It's probably worth a try. But I don't know. Who's going to do it? I don't really know any of them anymore. And they don't trust anybody."

They floated. Drops of water ran in slow crystals off the end of Louise's paddle and smacked the surface of the green-black water. The river was wide and slow. She could see peeled sticks of alder, left by beavers, lying on the edge of the thick gray mud. There were trails down to the water made by cattle and deer and elk, who paraded with great dignity and care through the brushy corridors under the dim shade from the huge cottonwoods.

"I don't know," Becky said again. "You know I'll do whatever I can to help. But mostly I think there's nothing you can do but wait for it all to balance out. Sometimes the shitheads win. But things have to even out sometime. We have to believe that, you know. Otherwise, things would just be too unbelievably depressing."

"But we have to do something ..."

"No, we don't," Becky turned on her. "No we don't. We don't have to do anything. We can sit in this goddamn boat and starve to death. We can go eat. Or we can go to town and parade up and down main street with signs or maybe we could blow up Sam Edward's house. We can do any damn thing. But we don't have to do anything. Except try and have some kind of life that we want. We can do what we want, goddammit. Not what we have to do — what we want!"

Louise said nothing, only watched Becky, who picked up the paddle, shook herself and said, normally, "Now come on. Let's try and enjoy ourselves. And I won't lecture anymore. But only if you quit being such a down-in-the-mouth pain-in-the-ass chicken-livered sad sack. Okay?"

Louise couldn't manage to laugh. But she smiled. She even managed a meagre grimacing snort before she picked up her paddle.

"Am I really like that?" she asked.

"Damn right," Becky grinned. "Having you around makes me feel smart. Now kindly paddle a bit so we get there before midnight."

They made it to the point, hauled the canoe out of the water, lit a fire and ate Becky's food and Louise's too. Then they lay on their backs, watching the stars and Louise had one of Becky's cigarettes. Becky sighed heavily.

"What?" said Louise cautiously. "Something's going on with you. I can tell."

"Oh, I'm just in love, is all. Again, goddammit. You think I'd learn. It's so embarrassing," Becky laughed, not her normal laugh but a nervous laugh — a giggle, like a schoolgirl. "I didn't want to tell you about it. You'll think I'm stupid. You'll think I'm out of control, again."

Louise was silent, stunned by Becky's revelation that she was afraid Louise might ever think badly of her. "But I've never thought that," she said.

"Oh, come on," said Becky. "What about all the times you've thought I should straighten up and get a real job? You never say anything. You just look at me. And what about all the good advice you've given me that I've never listened to? You, at least, have a place of your own and a somewhat reasonable life."

"A place of my own? I inherited that goddamn place, which, I might add, I have to share with Mark, who's only interested in chopping down the trees," she said. And then louder, much louder: "And I have a shitty life. A stupid shitty life. I'm lonely and scared most of the time, and I'm trying to figure out what to do with myself the other half. What's so great about that?"

"And money in the bank," Becky persisted.

"Which I blackmailed out of my crooked ex-husband," Louise suddenly giggled. Becky laughed too.

"A beer," she said. "I need a beer. We need beer. Maybe lots of beer. Maybe that's what's wrong with us. No beer and too many fucked up men."

They had a beer each and another cigarette. They buried the butts in the wet sand and then they stripped off their clothes and went swimming. Louise turned on her back in the water; the water flowed over her breasts and belly and suddenly she was flushed with desire — not for anyone, not even for sex, but just desire — a lust so huge and consuming that it encompassed everything around her, the willows dipping and nodding from the creek bank, the tiny minnows nibbling at the hairs on her legs, the water and the stones under the water, the earth under the stones, the roots and tendrils of plants, the cottonwood trees, the blackberries coming ripe along the fencerows, the sweet plants and food from her garden, the eroded shrunken breasts of the mountains.

She turned around and around, lolling in the water, amazed at its silken texture on her skin. Becky suddenly came up beneath her and grabbed her legs. Louise squealed and splashed her and they wrestled, splashing each other until they were both out of breath and the water churned to chocolate soup around them. Then they went back to the shore and put on their clothes, hurrying because there were mosquitoes, now that it was completely dark. Then they launched the canoe and headed back up the current towards the sandbar and the waiting trucks.

"So, what's he like?" said Louise.

"What?"

"Who is he? You didn't bother to tell me."

"Well, he's great, actually. He's not from around here. But he's younger than me. He has red hair and a great body and he wants us to live together. He's even talking about kids but I told him to give it a rest. Kids, for god's sake. Me with kids?"

"I can see it," said Louise. "Makes sense to me. They'll be wild and stubborn and crazy like the rest of your family and every time you get tired of them, you'll just send them over to Marie's and she'll feed them millions of cookies and that would shut them up. Simple, see?"

"Oh, just great," said Becky. "And, with my luck, they'll all be boys like my brothers and grow up and cut down what's left of the trees."

"And besides," she added softly. "I'm just too scared to have kids."

"You? You're not scared of anything."

"Oh, yes, I am."

"Tell me."

"I'm scared of all kinds of things. I'm scared of bears when I'm treeplanting. I'm scared of driving on freeways. I'm scared of the stupid, sick, sad, mad mess this world is in and the fact that nothing, as far as I can see, makes much difference anymore, at least nothing I can figure out how to do."

Becky paused. "And, sometimes, I think I'm scared most to really look and see who I am. I mean, I know who I am: one of Marie and Mick's half-breed kids. Sure, I live here. Roots and chains and all. God, the shit we used to take in school. I guess that's one reason why our family hangs together like we do. At least we always had each other for backup ... and if we didn't, Marie would smack us all up alongside the head and demand to know why we were letting the goddamn family down. But what hell does it mean? I'm not white, I'm not Indian. Sometimes I'm one or the other. Some days, I'm so Indian it scares me, then some days I'm just another white girl with dark skin. So, I have a sort of life. I have an education that's never done me a damn bit of good and a stupid trailer beside a creek and a few clothes. I can get by. I know how to survive. That took me a while to figure out. I know lots of things. But I'm damned if I know what any of it means. You ever think about all this stuff?"

"All the time."

"So what are you afraid of?"

"Oh, shit," said Louise. "Lots of things. Everything. Falling out of a tree. My truck dying on a dark road late at night. Fires ... the phone ringing ... but, mostly, I think I'm afraid no one will love me and I'll never love anyone again, because I'm too stupid to make it work, because I don't understand, I never seem to understand, what's going on. I'm scared I'll just get old and crotchety and even lonelier than I am now. People do things I never expect. I thought when Susan said she loved me, she meant it. I thought I knew what she meant. But now it doesn't seem to have meant anything. So I go through life as this person that things happen to, and I'm always scrambling to catch up. And when I do things, I'm afraid they'll fuck up and then they do. So now I'm afraid to do things, to take chances. I'm afraid to leave here ... I don't even want to. How will I ever have a life? How will I ever know anything? But I'm not stupid. I do know things. I can learn. Sometimes I'm even smart.

"I want my own life," Louise added, after a while. "That's all. I want to decide what I want. It's that simple, I guess."

It was almost pitch black at the landing. A warm breeze, smelling of night and damp, came down off the mountains and shook the cottonwoods and ruffled the river into silver, so they could see it gleam in the starlight.

They landed the canoe, more by feel than sight, and together loaded it on the rack on the top of Becky's truck. Then they hugged goodnight — a long warm affectionate hug.

Louise drove home, still lost in the memory of the water sliding its cool silk over and around her skin, and wondering why she had ever been mad at Becky.

Chapter 21

Becky came over to Louise's the next evening and they tried to plan, tried to think of themselves as smart — not just two women who weren't quite sure what they were doing, but two grown-up people who were smarter than jerks who would be stupid enough to use kids to run drugs, stupid enough to not even know what the kids were doing with their precious parcels, passing them from hand to hand.

"Jeezus, it was dumb, eh? It doesn't even make sense, trusting kids with something like that," Louise said again. "I thought crooks would be smarter."

"These aren't crooks; they're just smalltown businessmen with peabrains trying to make an extra profit."

They went together to Celeste's and started by trying, again, to talk to Celia, but she turned sullen, insisted that she didn't know anything more than what she had already said and couldn't tell them anything. She twisted and turned on the chair in front of them like a hooked fish until they let her go. Louise felt like a bully.

"Look, I'm sorry, Celia," she said. "I just thought there might be something else, you know. Something that would make things a little clearer."

Celia shook her head. "I told you what happened," she said, casting a sullen glance at Becky. "You said you trusted me. You said you wouldn't tell nobody." She turned away and buried her head in a tattered magazine.

Louise felt even worse when Celeste asked her cheerfully if she had found out anything more. She didn't know what to tell Celeste. She couldn't figure out anything; she just knew who she owed promises to. She said something vague about rumours and gossip and left it at that.

Becky went to town by herself and made inquiries but came back shaking her head. "Maybe they're smarter than we thought or maybe no one is talking. The kids I used to know have grown up and hit the road or married and become respectable or some damn thing," she said. "But I did hear one weird thing. You know that hitchhiker who disappeared, somewhere north of here? Well, they found a body, down a gully. The news is all over town. Nobody knows how the guy died or anything. But now the town is full of silly rumours, none of which are going to help us much. They're saying he was found with drugs on him, or that he died of an overdose or something. It's got people's attention."

"But what's it got to do with our problem?"

"Maybe nothing. Probably nothing. It's just more weirdness, is all. And in a town so full of churches. At least the police are involved now. Maybe they'll stumble over something that's lying right under their red noses. My, my. Whatever will happen next? And in the meantime, we have another problem."

"What's that?"

"What to do with you?"

"Me?" Louise echoed, astonished. "I'm all right. I'm getting by."

"No, you're not," said Becky.

"Says who?"

"Says me and Celeste and Marie, who, God knows, is always invincibly and unutterably right about these things. She says you're too skinny and you're unhappy and lonely and you should go away for a bit, meet some new friends, travel, have some fun. Which, I seem to recall, you have mentioned doing every now and again. She said to tell you if that Susan girl ever comes by again, to bring her over for a visit."

"Oh, my God," said Louise. "What did she mean by that?"

"Oh, nothing gets by Marie, you know that. No secret is safe around her."

"Oh shit," Louise whispered. She put her face in her hands.

"Oh, come on, it's okay," Becky said impatiently. "I don't know what you're so worried about. Nobody would make a big fuss, if they knew. You could be our token gay person."

"Yeah," Louise said, "but I don't want them to know. It's nobody's business. I don't want them looking at me and trying to figure me out, like I'm some kind of freak. I'm not into explanations or defending myself."

"Okay, okay," Becky said, "but I thought you were making plans to leave anyway."

"I don't want to go away anymore," said Louise. "I like it here fine. I have no problems, tell Marie that. Tell her not to worry about me. Tell her I'm all grown up and settled down and now I even have money. So: No problems. Just tell her that for me, okay?"

"Tell her yourself," said Becky. "You couldn't prove it by me. Strikes me you're kind of spinning your wheels, aren't you? Jeezus, you're letting this Celia thing really get to you. You act like you're obsessed with it. It's not really your problem."

"It sure as hell is," Louise snapped. "They made it my problem. They burned my house. They tried to wreck my life."

"You don't know that for sure," Becky pointed out reasonably. "All you really know is what Celia's told you. I think you're just putting things off 'cause you're scared. There's your own life to deal with, instead of everybody else's. Hey, I have to go. I'll catch you later."

"Sure, fine, thanks," Louise muttered.

But after Becky left, the trailer walls rang noisily with questions and accusations. She wandered into the bedroom and kicked at the mess of papers on the floor and wandered out again and snapped the TV on and off and looked out the darkening windows at her dim reflection and the valley beyond. Reverberations of what Becky had said, and all the varying resonances of the word *failure*, banged and and echoed in the hollow chambers of her body and crawled along her nerves like caterpillars. They stared back at her from the blank windows.

"I am not spinning my goddamn wheels. I'm living my life. That's all," she said out loud. She took her heavy body into the kitchen and made tea and soup. The tea tasted of ashes. She poured the soup into the compost bucket and went back to lay on the cushions in front of the TV. She watched without seeing.

It wasn't what Becky had said that disturbed her; it was all the echoes of her own accusations coming back again and again, going around and around like voices trapped in a tunnel. She doubled over on the rug, holding her stomach, and rocked back and forth, staring at the phone. No one to call.

She went into the bedroom where the carved horse stood on the table, and picked it up and carried it into the living room and held onto it. She lay on the carpet, hugged the horse to her belly and stroked the smooth patina of the wood. She got out the knives she used for carving and held one to her arm, pushed, tried to push hard enough to draw blood — couldn't do it. Tried to jab at her wrists but pulled back at the last minute.

She stood up, took the horse outside to the woodpile and set it down on the old mossy block of cottonwood that served her as a chopping block. She stood back, admired it, hated it — it's bright foolishness, meaning nothing. She picked up the axe and, using the blunt end, smashed the horse again and again until it was only splinters and wood dust. Then she went and sat, shivering, on the steps of the trailer, staring out over the valley. Becky might reconsider and come back. She thought of phoning Celeste but she couldn't imagine what to say. She went on sitting, shaking, with her arms wrapped around herself, holding in the tiny fluttering of warmth under her shirt.

Eventually, she dozed; then woke, shaking violently from cold. She went inside but didn't go into the bedroom. Instead, she curled up on the floor, pulled her coat over herself and lay there, still shaking in occasional spasms, until she drifted back to sleep.

When she woke up, she lay on the floor for a long time. Her body ached; it felt bruised, as if she had been hit by something. She crawled into the small shower cubicle and stood under the hot water until it ran cold. She had to go into the bedroom where the horse had been in order to change her clothes, but she didn't look at the bare place on the table. Instead, she pulled out her least-worn pair of blue jeans and a green sweater with no holes in it. She tied a scarf someone had given her around her neck and pulled her hair back into a respectable knot.

She felt very dull and very far removed from what she was doing. She looked in the mirror and a stranger peered at her from dull eyes. A loose hank of hair fell forward and she noticed, for the first time, a white curly hair protruding from the straight brown ones. She jerked it out, tucked the hair back behind her ears, went out to the truck and drove to the local sawmill. Celeste had said Sam Edwards was still working there.

When she got out of the truck, in front of the mill office, she stopped. Her belly cramped. She wasn't sure she could walk. The sawmill seemed like a nightmare of noise, machines, speed. Forklifts roared by, carrying lumber. Logging trucks rumbled in with enormous loads of logs. Men peered curiously at her but no one stopped or asked questions.

She went in the door. A receptionist stared at her with a blank look — she was no one Louise knew.

"Uh, I need to see Sam Edwards," she said.

The receptionist nodded and smiled. "Yeah, well, go on in," she said and went back to her typing.

Louise walked into the room and sat down. Sam Edwards was on the phone. He looked at her with no expression, then went back to his phone call. She waited and took a long look at him: He was tall and could have been distinguished looking, except for the net of red veins that laced his nose and cheeks and the potbelly that protruded over his belt.

He hung up the phone, looking at her with no sign of recognition. "Something I can do for you?" he asked.

"I'm Louise," she said. "Louise McDonald. We met at Stephen's."

"Oh yeah, right," he said, still uninterested.

"A friend suggested I talk to you."

"Yeah? About what?"

She hesitated, then said finally, "Something weird is going on in this town."

"What are you talking about? Look, lady, I got work to do. You got a complaint about logging or something, take it up with the foreman."

"No, it's not about logging. A friend of mine got busted for bringing coke through the border. She's only a kid, only thirteen. Someone set her up."

"Yeah, and I'm supposed to know something about this?"

"Yeah, apparently."

He started to stand up.

"Look," Louise said. "My house burned down, my best friends are in trouble, my ex-husband turns out to be not such a nice guy, and my life is a mess. I'm not very happy about any of it. I've been trying to figure it out. Someone told me to talk to you. So you can tell me, or I can just keep asking questions. Sooner or later I'll find out. This is just too small a town for this kind of shit. It's just the wrong kind of place to try to keep a secret."

He sat back down. "I don't know anything about any of this," he said.

"Some guy, some hitchhiker, got himself killed, north of town," she added. "They're saying he was carrying drugs. Seems like he got lost — fell off a rock or something."

Sam put his hands together, studying her. "So what do you want with me?" he said sullenly. "I don't know nothing. You're wasting your time. People who play around with drugs are not nice people, you know. Girls like you should stay home and play house and stick to what you know. Or you can get yourself in even bigger trouble. Get your friends in even bigger trouble."

"Okay," Louise said. "If that's the way you want to play it." She stood up.

You know," she added reflectively. "I never much liked this town. I never thought of it as much of a place, just an ordinary kind of community, with ordinary folks in it. But you got no right," she said vehemently, heat growing in her voice, "no right to be here, no right to do what you're doing, no right to try to wreck our lives. No right at all."

"Just get the hell out of here," he said. "Quit wasting my time making empty threats, you ugly dyke bitch."

She started to leave. Then she turned around. "You've got no right here," she said, deadly quiet. "You'll find out. It's you who is going to leave. You don't belong here. You'll find out." Then she stomped out before she lost her voice to fear. The people in the office stared as she went by them. The office door crashed hard behind her. She got in the truck, slammed the door, started the motor, spun her tires on the gravel and drove onto the highway. She started towards the turn-off that led back to home — to safety and refuge — then slowed down, pulled a u-turn in the middle of the road and headed back towards town.

When she stopped at the RCMP station, she was still shaking. She tried to recover the protective remoteness of earlier in the morning — it had taken her this far — but her legs buckled under her as she got out of the truck. Then she pulled herself back up straight.

She had no idea what the police would think of her story. Maybe they would find some way of making her guilty and excusing Stephen and Sam. No doubt she was guilty, somehow. But still, it was what you did, knowing someone had broken the law. You told the police. On the other hand, the police were never your friends. They gave you speeding tickets and made you fix your tired and fading truck when you barely had enough money to walk from one day to the next; they loomed only as a vague and threatening presence which made everything people did to survive seem barely possible — growing a little dope, drinking a little too much, driving a little too fast.

Somehow, she made it out of the truck and into the police station. A receptionist stared at her blankly when she asked to see someone, then disappeared and came back with a piece of paper.

"Please fill this in," she snapped then went back to her desk. Louise stared hopelessly at the paper, then stood up.

"But I just need to talk to somebody," she said. "I just ..." she stopped. There was no such thing as anonymous in this town, which they both knew. "Uh ... Unofficially," she said finally, hoping that was the right word.

The receptionist glared at her. Then she stood up without a word and disappeared again.

Louise sat down, then stood up again. She studied the pictures of children who had long since disappeared, and the rack of pamphlets on drinking and driving and various programs promising to help her with her problems. She read through two of them. They didn't seem useful. She tried to imagine phoning someone in an office somewhere and explaining her life to them.

A policeman came through the door. It was the same man who had talked with her and Celeste last winter. She followed him into a back room with a desk and sat down while he closed the door. Now she felt simple terror enfold her with wings of great strength and power; it was almost, but not quite, enough to lift her entirely out of herself, out of the room, out of the situation.

The policeman looked at her, plainly waiting for her to speak.

"This is a long story," she said. "It probably sounds really crazy but I thought I had to tell someone. Maybe it won't even make any sense." She looked around the office. There were pictures of a woman with two children, and of a horse, on the policeman's desk. Maybe he liked horses.

She looked back at him. *He's just a man*, she thought. *He has a wife and two kids and a horse.*

"Do you want some coffee?" he asked. He had a nice ordinary face — a familiar kind of face. He had sandy hair and a little moustache and blue eyes and he was probably a kind father — although how could you tell? She nodded. He went out and came back quickly with a styrofoam cup of very bitter coffee.

She told him the story. She started with Celia and tried not to leave anything out — the phone calls, her burned house, Celeste and Harold, the morning at Stephen's, Sam Edwards, the scarred boy. In the end, she had to leave some things out. She had promised Celia. While she was speaking, her voice was tinny and distant. She couldn't tell if she was actually making sense. At least the policeman listened and didn't interrupt, although several times he frowned and he tapped a pencil on the desk and once he impatiently moved his tiny desk calendar to a more prominent position and then back again. She thought she was boring him and tried to finish the story faster so she could leave and he could forget she had ever bothered him. He could go back to his nice tidy life of filling in forms and giving out speeding tickets.

When she stopped talking, he stretched out in his chair and made a little steeple with his hands. Frowning, he said, "But you're not here to lay any charges, or make a complaint, is that right?"

"Yes," said Louise sullenly. "I just thought ... I thought maybe, well, maybe something like this would be useful, I thought ... well, I don't know, maybe I thought you could use it to connect things together. God, I don't know what I thought. I had to tell someone. I couldn't handle it anymore by myself. I didn't know what to do. I still don't."

"Yeah, well," he said, still looking at his hands. "It might be useful. Hard to tell at this point. These things always take time. And right now, we've got nothing we can waltz into court with, you understand?"

Louise nodded.

"I take it you'll be around for a while if we need a statement?" he asked.

"Well, no," she heard herself say. "I'm thinking of going back to university this fall."

"Well, we can always get you back here if we need you," he said. "Tough luck losing your house like that. How are you managing?"

"Someone gave me a travel trailer to live in."

He nodded. They were both silent.

"How's the girl, what's-her-name, making out?"

"Celia," said Louise. "She's okay. She's a good kid. She comes riding with me. I think she'll be okay."

"Kids these days. Got a lot to deal with," he said and shook his head. They were silent again. Then, as if moved by mutual silent agreement, they both stood at the same time. He stuck out his hand and she shook it.

"Thanks," he said. "We'll be in touch. Sorry we can't be more helpful at the moment. But thanks for coming in. Appreciate it. You be careful, eh?"

Louise nodded and backed out of the office, almost running into the door. She got lost trying to find the front door of the building, but finally made it and let herself outside into the hot sunshine. She had forgotten all about the outside world during those endless minutes in the office with no windows. The sun shone hot on the pavement, on the variety of colours of the vehicles parked on both sides of the street, on the mirrored plate glass window of the store opposite the police station. The sun shimmered and, in spite of it, she was cold in her sweater; she rubbed her clammy hands on her belly under the sweater and then climbed into the familiar, cluttered, stinking hot interior of her truck. She sat there with her head on the steering wheel until she felt strong enough to drive. Then went home.

Becky was waiting for her on the trailer steps. Louise sat down beside her and put her head on Becky's shoulder and stayed like that for a long while before she told her about her morning.

Chapter 22

Louise waited for something to happen. She got up the next morning and went to work, clipped tree branches all day, came home, waited. The phone didn't ring. The week dragged its slow, lazy length by, the sun shone every day, flowers bloomed, life rattled and sang on its way all around her.

On Friday night, Mark phoned.

"Hey, didja hear the news?" he said. There was a lot of background noise, and Louise realized he must be in a bar. "Harold's buddy — Sam Edwards, the one giving him a hard time — he's disappeared. Apparently, there's a whole pile of money missing from the sawmill accounts. Pretty slick, that dude, eh? All kinds of talk going around town. I guess the guy's done this before. Some say he was mixed up in all kinds of other shit. Dunno if you can believe half the crap that's going around. Some even figure the mill might go down. Anways, thought I'd let you know. Take it easy, Lou. Come on over Sunday, if you're not doing nothing."

Louise hung up the phone and went outside, down to the pasture fence. The horses came nickering to the fence. She looked at the sky. There was time yet. She went back inside, phoned Celia.

"Come on over," she said. "Let's go riding."

Celeste drove Celia over. Louise had the horses saddled and waiting. "Let's go to the big pasture again," she said. They went out the driveway, down the hill and through the network of old logging roads, then through the gate into the large flat willow-speckled stretch of marsh and meadow that stretched beside the river. The horses jigged and danced and snatched at their bits at the sight of the long flat opening.

"Wanta run?" she yelled to Celia.

In response, Celia kicked Bigger and, at the same moment, George dug in his heels and rocketed off. They flashed together, side by side, the horses stretched out, Louise and Celia leaning forward over the horses' necks, urging them on, flying over hollows and logs and past willow thickets and cottonwoods, faster and faster, their mouths open, hair whipping in their eyes. A flock of geese that had been feeding on the grass took off and flew in front of them, black shapes in the gathering evening. Far away in the back of Louise's head was the thought that this was foolishly dangerous — it was too dark and the footing was uneven and … who cared? She leaned over, yelled at Bigger and grinned at the blur that was Celia. They ran on and on, while the geese circled, crying, over their heads and the horses pounded their joy of flying into the soft turf. The rest of the world was left far, far behind in the darkness under the trees. Finally, they pulled up, the horses puffing and snorting, but still wanting to run. Celia and Louise looked at each other and grinned.

"One more," yelled Louise, and they took off through the black soft night.

It was true what Becky had predicted: Stephen got his. Louise didn't even hear about it until later. Becky had invited her — actually, Becky had ordered her — to go to the city with her. While they were there, Becky dragged her to a student counselling service at the one of the universities. Louise looked blindly at the courses and degrees and months of sweaty, lonely effort in front of her and thought of her yard — the cool downdraft off the mountains in the evening, the apple trees covered with fruit. Then, she signed the form.

"It's only a year to finish your degree," Becky said encouragingly. "And then you could do damn near anything you wanted."

But Louise felt as if she had just willingly signed herself into jail for a year.

"I'll have a degree," she said bitterly, "but I still won't have a job and what good will that do?"

"Oh, you'll be so much more fun to argue with, my dear," Becky laughed.

They argued all the way to the university coffee shop where Louise sat, dazed, while students of all sizes, ages and colours ran in and out, carrying books and looking sure of themselves.

"I don't think I can do this, Beck," Louise said desperately. "I'd never fit in here. These people know what they're doing. They belong here. They're not some dusty old hill farmer with mud on her boots."

"Okay, fine," said Becky. "I'm going to show you something."

"What now?" Louise was peevish.

"Just come with me. We're going to the mall. You got that fancy new credit card of yours?"

At the mall, Becky dragged Louise inside a store full of young skinny women who had hair done in odd shapes and colours.

"Now," said Becky, handing her clothes. "Try these on. And these and this. Put them on all together. Put this over the tee-shirt and tie this around your waist. And socks. We can't forget new socks."

They bought the clothes and Becky dragged Louise to a hair salon and told the stylist how to cut it. Louise slouched, dazed, in her chair.

"Okay," Becky said. "To the washroom." The washroom in the mall was huge. Women marched in and out in a steady stream. Louise changed into the new clothes and came out and scowled at the mirror. It was her, but it wasn't.

"See," said Becky. "It's all camouflage. It's like jungle warfare. They can't see you now. They can't tell anything about you. You can be anyone or no one. The great thing is that no one cares and the awful thing is that no one cares. Besides, every single person in this mall is wondering if they look okay, or if they're good enough to make it into some exclusive little area marked normal, or if they're still just on the border looking in. There's people who truly don't give a shit, like us, but it just saves us a lot of time and trouble if we wear the camouflage."

"But I did this before. I did this with Stephen. It never worked. It just made me feel like a phony, a prostitute. I was pretending to be someone even I didn't want to know." Louise looked at the mirror again. The person there looked different, older, more sure of herself.

"It's cheating," she said. "Buy some new clothes, spend some money, be a new person. It doesn't really change anything."

"Yeah, you're right," said Becky. "But there's games and there's games. You just choose which ones you want to play or if you want to play at all. C'mon Louise, time to play a little," Becky said cheerfully. They went across the street to a big hotel and ordered coffee. Becky joked with the waiter. Louise sat where she could continue to catch glimpses of herself in the mirror. Her new clothes were gold, with soft greens and muted purples. She sulked over her expensive pastry. It was still cheating. And she didn't like cappuccino. She liked the bakery, puffy white donuts and tea.

"Peachy!" Becky laughed. "You look peachy. Good enough to smooch with. Wanta go to a gay bar tonight?"

"No!" said Louise, startled out of sneaking looks at herself in the mirror behind the bar. "No, I goddamn well don't. You never quit, do you? Isn't it enough that I'm sitting here tarted up like some fancy monkey with my hair stuck together and stinking of perfume? Isn't it enough that you're trying to destroy my last piece of integrity. No, I'm not going to a gay bar."

"But she might be there."

"I don't want to see her … you know that. Leave off, already."

"You might meet someone."

"And then what would I do? Drag her back to the farm with me? Ask her to help me clean horseshit off the pasture?"

"No, just go have some fun, for a change. You're a prude, aren't you?"

"No," Louise snapped. "I am not a goddamn prude. Life is just fine without sex. It's a hell of a lot less confusing. Look at you, buzzing around what's-his-name. Acting like it matters what he thinks."

"You miss it, don't you? You miss having someone around, right?"

"Well, of course … " Louise started to say, then stopped. "Sometimes," she said softly, "sometimes in the middle of the night, it's true, I want someone there. But then I think I might not want them there in the morning. And yeah, sometimes, yeah, I do — I get this great raging desire to just go out and find someone and have sweaty, raunchy all-night sex … and then what happens? Do we have to have a relationship after that, or what? Do I want one? And can I live with that at home? Would they let me? I know you think everyone would be okay but I still don't know how to handle it. I want some parts of the deal; or I want it all, I can't decide — and, at home, I don't have many choices. When Susan left, I felt like I was crossing a bridge I hadn't known existed. It was like being a teenager all over again. She woke up these new parts of me; showed me something I hadn't known existed. And then she disappeared and it all stopped, just like that. Sure, I'd like to know more. I don't even know if it was just Susan. She was so gorgeous. Maybe I'm not … " she stopped.

"There's that word," Becky said. "Lesbian. Maybe you could practice it."

"It's an ugly word. I don't like it."

"But it's also a real word for a lot of people."

"But I don't know if I want to be like them, if I even want to know them. I don't want their label, anymore than I want any other labels. I want my own label. I'm just a dumb farmer. What's wrong with that?"

"Nothing. Except it's not all true either, is it? You're a lot more than that. Look at you. You're a gorgeous woman in great clothes sitting in an expensive hotel with your half-breed best friend who has her many degrees in a buckskin pouch on her back. And who knows what stories these waiters walk around with? Look at the black guy over there. Maybe he's from Africa or Jamaica. Maybe he was born here. Maybe he likes it or hates it. How will we ever know? All we can see is his face. And behind him is the culture that made him, and the genetics that made his parents and the history of colonialization and slavery and whatever other gross things have happened so he could end up for a while as a waiter in a high-priced hotel waiting on us. See, life is so interesting."

They stayed in in the city for another two days, but Louise got increasingly restless.

"How do people stand it here?" she said. "There's no air, no ground. Everything is made of straight lines. It's so goddamn ugly."

"Go to the park," Becky snapped. She was busy buying supplies. She and Lucas, her new man, had decided to set themselves up in the catering business for the summer. They had leased a kitchen at one of the marina resorts down the river, where Americans came in their pleasure cruisers, tied up for the weekend and went home again. Becky was going to get her Mom to make pies and cakes for the venture. Privately, Louise gave both the business and the relationship about another six weeks.

"I hate the park. It's too small. It's the city's token idea of what a real woods might look like."

"Go shopping. Buy some more clothes."

"I can't go shopping without you. I don't know what to buy."

"Then just wander. Look at the city. Buy more books. That always makes you happy."

Which it did. So Louise, dressed in her new clothes, spent the afternoon in the bookstore and even went to the teashop at the art gallery (which didn't serve donuts) and took out her new books — her jeweled treasures — and wrote her name in each one. When she got back, Becky was cursing over the phone at her new love, who, it appeared, had bought exactly the wrong kind of bread mixer.

Chapter 23

The next day, Louise and Becky left for home. After the long day's drive, Louise fell out of the car, stiff and dazed; and the next morning she got up and strolled around her flowers and plants and fruit trees and visited the horses and cleaned her tidy trailer — which had somehow gotten dusty while she was away — and then sat on the steps watching the sunset, wondering why it all felt so dull after the city. She thought about the newness of things there, the stores reeking of newness and promise: Buy me. Life will change.

"Have I done something wrong?" she wondered. She felt like a traitor, treacherously guilty. The butchered stumps from the hillside above her leaked the tang of pine resin into the damp air. But that was partly atoned for: She'd spent the better part of a week planting new trees on the hillside, lugging buckets of water to settle them in. It was the best she could do.

The next morning, she took the horses out. She wouldn't sell them — she'd give them to Celia to look after. It would be good for Celia to have the responsibility. They were lovely, lovely horses. She leaned over Bigger's smooth brown neck. He plodded on, but not obliviously. She could see him flicking his ears, wondering what she wanted, whether he was being given signals he should pay attention to or just signals he could safely ignore. She straightened up. Bigger had his own set of rules and strategic behavours which didn't include trying to figure out his depressed mistress. Since she was his rider she should behave like one. They had a brisk canter along the road by the river, but even that didn't break the mood of dullness into which she had fallen.

When she got home, she unsaddled, got in her truck and drove straight to Celeste's.

"Where in the hell have you been?" Celeste snapped, happily pouring immense mugs of coffee and hauling out a cake which had seen better days. "You've missed all the fun here. It's been just wonderful. Stephen has bit the dust at last. God got him, and a damn good thing too. Maybe there is such a thing as cosmic justice, eh?"

"Celeste, slow down, sit down, and explain this all to me in words of one syllable. And cut me some cake. I'm starving. What else do you have to eat?"

"There's some leftover beef stew and biscuits. Want that? And, oh yeah," she said, rummaging in the fridge, "there's some salad from last night. Here," she said, loading the table with plastic containers of food. "Here, eat, you must have just about starved to death in the city. It's so expensive there. And of course, Becky never worries about little minor details like food."

"So, what happened to Stephen?" Louise said, with her mouth full. "A meteorite fall on his house, or what?"

"Better," said Celeste, still beaming. "You know, Bimbette, that blond he had working for him. She's suing him for sexual harassment. Said he made her sleep with him to keep her job. She's suing him for money, which will, of course, hurt him the most. It's such a great story. It's all over town. People are lining up to take sides. Poor old Stephen, I bet he stays away from women for good after this. First you, now Bimbette."

"Yeah, but he's still getting away with arson and drug dealing. That's more serious than chasing Bimbette around his office a few times. Besides, she's lying through her teeth. I saw her at his house. She wasn't forced to be there. She looked at me like I had leprosy."

"Honey, you're supposed to take the feminist side here. You're supposed to be on the side of Women. And now you won't even take poor Bimbette's word for what happened. Shame on you. What kind of bullshit is that? Maybe he really did threaten her. Who knows? Maybe there's a lot more to this story than meets the eye."

"What, you think she might know something about some of this other shit?"

"Worth asking her, since she appears to have switched sides."

"Maybe."

"I'll come with you," said Celeste, "if you're too chicken to go on your own. Maybe we could get Becky to help too."

"Yeah right, we'll confront her with a crowd and she'll break down and tell us all the truth, eh? Fat chance."

"Worth a try, though."

"Yeah, worth a try."

And so they did go, the three of them: Harold, Celeste and Louise, tarted up in her new clothes to compete with the lacquered polish of Bimbette. The next evening, they drove to the address they'd been given by a friendly gossip at Celeste's church. They held a whispered frantic consultation in the car. Finally, after many combinations were discussed, it was decided that Louise and Harold would go in. After all, they had been most directly threatened.

Louise marched up the sidewalk feeling doom in her stomach. She reminded herself that it was just Bimbette. Probably just a nice normal woman she had never had a chance to get to know — a woman wronged. They should all be on her side. Why was she so terrifying? Perhaps just that lacquered normalcy, her ability to look at Louise and reflect back an image of someone worth despising.

Louise rang the doorbell. Harold coughed and shuffled his feet beside her. There was some noise and yelling inside. Finally the door was opened by a very small, very blond girl.

Two other children, also blond but even smaller, peeked around behind the first.

"Ummm, is your Mommy at home?" Louise ventured. She wondered if they had the wrong house.

"Mummy," they wailed in unison, running towards the back of the house. Bimbette appeared, looking sullen, her hair in curlers but her face still carefully made up. Louise wondered if she slept in makeup.

"We'd, uh, like to talk to you about Stephen," she said.

Bimbette's face went through several changes of expresson. She looked angry, then puzzled, then finally she motioned them inside to chairs in the living room. Her living room was tidy — full of cheap furniture, plants, kid's toys, women's fashion magazines, faded plastic flowers. It was a room where someone had made an effort but hadn't succeeded. The rug was an ancient faded green, curling at the edges in between the tacks that had been driven into the floor to hold it down.

"We're sorry about your trouble with Stephen," Louise ventured gently. "I guess it must be pretty hard on you."

"I don't know what they think I'm supposed to feed these damn brats — air and water, I suppose. I don't get no money 'til the damn case is settled, and now I ain't got a car. They come and took that away this morning. Maybe welfare will give me something. I dunno. I ain't been up there yet, but I'll have to go tomorrow." She lit a cigarette.

She didn't seem either angry or sad, so much as utterly resigned to the way things went in life.

"So, can you tell us what happened?" Louise asked. "I mean, if you want to talk about it."

"Well, you ought to know what's he's like, seeing as how he's your ex. You must have gone through it; he always did get around. So, one night, he started talking about his needs — nothing about my needs or nothing, but that's men, what the hell. So I thought, hey, he's a nice guy, got a little money, nice big house, no wife in sight, what's wrong with it? Which was okay until one night I told him I had to go home, didn't have no babysitter or nothing, and he gets real mad, says if I ever quit going with him, or if I start seeing other men, I'll be out of a job so fast it'll make my head spin. And furthermore," she stopped and pursed her lips over this word, "furthermore, he says, I won't get no other job in this one-horse town neither. So I says, what do I get out of the deal, apart from a lousy fuck now and then? So he got real mad and threw me out. Well, I learned just a bit more than he thinks, working in that office. So I called your lawyer — you know, the one in the next town — and he says we got a good case for sexual harassment and we can get some more money out of Stevie the wonder boy. Guess he figures he's found himself a golden milk cow. But what do I care, long as I can get a bit of money and another job? I got these little ones to think of."

"Where's your husband?" Louise said, still softly.

"Oh, probably drunk in some oil camp in Alberta. He sends money sometimes, comes by to see the kids. He's okay. He's just not very, whatdyacallit, domesticated or nothing like that."

"I'm sorry," said Louise. "I don't even know your name."

"Tiffany," said Tiffany.

Tiffany," she said, "do you know Harold here?"

Tiffany shook her head.

"Well," Louise plowed on, "his daughter Celia got caught carrying drugs across the border. Some other kids just handed them to her and ran. That's what she says and I believe her. She says the kids got the drugs from a guy named Sam Edwards, and he's a friend of Stephen's. Did you ever hear them talking about anything like that?"

Tiffany's face closed down like a window shade. "Naw," she said. "I know Sam Edwards. He wouldn't do nothing like that."

"Well, if you really know him, you know he's split town with the assets from the sawmill. So he probably would do something like that. Tiffany, did you know my house burned down?"

"Yeah, I heard about it."

"I think the fire was deliberately set and the fire marshall thinks so as well. He just can't prove it. And, a while back, Harold here got a letter from Sam Edwards when he was at the sawmill threatening to have Harold fired. I've already talked to the cops and they say they need more information. Tiffany, these are not nice people. They're not nice at all and they're not worth protecting."

"I ain't into protecting nobody except myself and my kids," Tiffany flashed. "Not you. Not them. I ain't taking sides."

"Tiffany, you want your kids growing up in a town like this? Where things get covered up and people get away with a lot of bad shit? Is that what you want? We're on the same side here. I don't want to cause you any trouble ... I just want you to tell me if you heard anything."

"Sure, I heard lots of stuff. Doesn't mean I know if it's true. I never saw any drugs." She paused. "Look," she said. "I got just this one chance. I got to prove my case, get a little extra money and get another job. I don't got a lot of choices here. I figure if I get mixed up in the shit you're looking at, I could get in big trouble. I can't afford no more trouble. I got three bundles of it and a whole lapful of other shit I can't figure out what to do with. Like how to get another goddamn car with no money and no credit ... nobody in this town is going to testify against those guys anyway, even if you found something out. Everyone is scared. Everyone is just trying to get by and have a normal life, y'know?"

"Yeah, I know," said Louise. "That's what I want. That's what Harold and his family want. We all got mixed up in this crap by accident and now we're trying to figure our own way out. Maybe you're right. Maybe the best thing is to duck and let it all fly by. I don't know. But thanks anyway. We'll let you know if anything turns up that will help your case. You never know."

Louise and Harold said their goodnights, left and got back in the car. In her mind, Louise kept seeing the tattered green shag rug and the faces of the three little girls. Wonder what their names are, she thought. My god, if only a name could make life simple. If only life lived up to the promise of a name like Tiffany.

"Goddamn," said Harold. "Seems like I been too easy on that guy. That Stephen. Him and his smooth talk. I always figured you women were a bit hard on him. Guess I figured wrong. You know, seems like maybe me and a bunch of the other guy oughta take a few matters into our own hands."

"Harold, you stay out of it," said Celeste crossly. "Now that's just what this family needs, you going and getting busted for smacking around a town lawyer. Yeah, that would do us a world of good, for sure — get our names and mugs plastered all over the goddamn paper right beside his."

"Now, Celeste, honey, I only meant maybe it's time we oughta take a kind of more active role in this. Seems to me we been kind of letting Louise take the brunt of this and she's got her own life to deal with. Now she's going to school and all ... she's got her own stuff to do."

"Oh, sure," said Celeste. "I know your more active role. You'd go blundering around, maybe get yourself beat up or killed or stumble into something you can't handle."

"Celeste, I only meant ..."

"I know what you meant and where the hell were you when I was holding your daughter's hand and trying to pull her back to some kind of normal life? Outside under a goddamn bejeezly truck, that's where you spend half your life while I'm trying to get food on the table and clean up the Christly mess and keep some order and make sure at least some of the kids get to school once in a while with their homework done."

Harold's face darkened. "Well, maybe you ain't done such a goddamn perfect job all the time, or we wouldn't be in this mess," he said.

"And maybe if you had helped out a little more, we wouldn't be in this mess. What kind of place do we live in, anyway, where kids can get drugs at the blink of an eye, and lawyers can't keep their pants on long enough to stay out of trouble? Next thing you know, we'll have every other kind of trouble here, crooks moving in from the city. Crooks attract crooks ... that's what I always figure. I thought this was some kind of moral, safe place to raise our kids, and just look at it."

"Well, it's a hell of a lot better here than in the city. You ain't got all them gay people spreading AIDS."

"Oh, for God's sake, Harold. Gay people are just people like anyone else. I'm talking about real crooks, people who break the law. You wouldn't know a gay person if one came up and ruffled your non-existent hair."

Louise looked out the window. Celeste stared straight ahead at the glare of the road in the headlights. They drove the rest of the way home in tight, tense silence. After Louise got out of the truck, she heard their voices begin again, even over the roar of the motor. They were shouting at each other as they drove towards home.

Chapter 24

Louise began to feel a bit left out of things after that. She heard one day that Stephen was sporting a black eye around town. Then she heard that his house was for sale and he was leaving. She heard that he had lost the court case. She thought of phoning Tiffany but decided against it. It wasn't worth it, and her sympathy would be useless and misplaced anyway.

But then there was an announcement that Stephen had accepted a new post with an important law firm, somewhere else — in some city, suitably far away. The local paper did a write up on him, in which his civic virtures and donations to charity were strongly stressed. The local paper also periodically announced in prim and proper tones that it had a policy against printing the results of court cases unless they were of major importance — which, of course, meant that no one who was important who got into trouble ever got his, or occasionally her, name in the paper.

Louise did see Tiffany, a few weeks later, working behind the counter in the bakery. After that, Louise stopped going to the bakery, regretting her addiction to donuts. She wondered how someone supported three kids on the salary she earned from working in a bakery. But then, a few days later, Louise saw Tiffany driving a new red Mustang, so perhaps she had other ways of getting by. Fortunately, she also disappeared out of the bakery around the same time so Louise could safely resume her habit of tea, two sugar donuts and a half-hour over the big city papers.

Louise went on working for George, even though there wasn't much to do at the height of summer. She thinned apples, mowed grass, even weeded his garden. After work she came home, turned the sprinklers on the lawn and made herself some dinner — something disgusting and simple, like rice with tuna fish or noodle soup with lots of onions. She ate it while watching the lights from the town twinkle and shift across the valley. From a distance, it looked like jeweled lace strung delicately around the crested hill. The lights were reflected in the river and against the misty thin clouds which drifted over from the low mountains.

"It's just a place," she'd said, with a shrug to Becky. "It's probably not much different than any other place." But she wondered if that was true. She'd find out when she moved.

She had tried to give the trailer back to George, but he wouldn't take it. "Naw ... Just leave it there," he said. "You're going to need it when you come back."

"But George," Louise said, teasing. "What if I don't come back? What if I turn into one of them big city women, eh, with a great job and a new car?"

"Aw, you'll come back," he said with disgusted conviction. "You'll get your fancy education but then you'll come back. That's a good thing to do. Everbody should have a good education. Then, when you come back — yah, maybe you do some good in this town. Maybe you show us old folks a thing or two. You'll come back. Time you planted a new orchard up at your Dad's place. That was the best land for peaches and apricots I ever seen. Grapes there too, long time ago. Raspberries. Long time ago. Your Dad, he let all that go. Said there wasn't no market for it. Couldn't make a go of it. Yah, but there's a market now, I think, all these new people moving in. Peaches and apricots. You come back, I'll help you replant, eh? Get you good rootstock, show you grafting, old style, not this crap you get in the nurseries."

"That's a hell of a deal, George," she said softly. "Thanks. Thanks a lot."

"You a good worker," he said, waving his arms. "Can't find good workers. Bunch of bums these days. Goddam hippie bums. But you a good worker." He wandered off, muttering to himself.

Louise stood still. "There are some moments," she thought, "when life makes sense. Just a few. And this is one of them. I should remember this."

She looked around George's dusty gray yard: there was the red barn with the sagging roof, the tractors and spraying equipment parked side by side, the distant smell of herbicide mingled with hot dust, diesel from the tractors and the sweet pungency of drying hay.

Then she shrugged, picked up the shears she was using to thin the rapidly swelling green apples on George's trees and went back to work. She didn't have to remember it. It would never change. In one or two or ten years, she could come back again and George, the yard, the apple trees and the mountains in the distance would never change. Some things could be relied on.

On a sunny August day, two weeks before school was due to start, she finally, reluctantly realized that it was time to get ready to leave. She knew she would be leaving in a state of terror. Without Becky to help this time, she still had to face the city, find a place to stay and get herself strong and organized enough to make it back inside the university walls.

Even as she packed up the trailer and stored yet more stuff in Celeste's basement, nothing in her believed that she was actually going to do this. Nothing in her believed that one morning soon she would wake up to something other than her familiar view and her familiar routine and her familiar life.

Leaving her life behind was far too easy. Celeste and Harold were glad to keep the horses, hoping they might keep Celia at home more often. Lately, Celia had begun hanging around the 7-11 until later hours, and one or the other of them usually drove reluctantly into town at night to fetch her home.

No one protested or held her back. No one said, *you're crazy. Stay here.* Instead, they mostly echoed George, so that even she was forced to think that, perhaps, finally, she was doing a good thing.

"When you come back, we'll talk about building you a new house," Mark had said. "Lately, Janet's been saying how nice it is out at the farm and how crowded the town is getting. Who knows? You might have us for neighbours, eh?"

"I don't think Janet's much of a farm girl," Louise said, managing to be polite and calm and distant instead of screaming wildly at the idea.

"Well, she could learn. And it'd be good for the boys. Remember the fun we had, eh, Lou? Running in the woods, building hideouts and all."

"Kids don't do that anymore, Mark. They watch TV and hang out at 7-11."

But Mark was lost in some dream reverie of his own. "Yeah, let 'em learn a little independence. Remember how Dad gave us those hatchets and we used them to build forts. Jeez. We had a lot of fun sometimes, Lou. When Mom wasn't bitchin' about the place or the old man wasn't going on about money."

Louise sighed. The idea of Mark's kids loose in the woods with hatchets gave her the shivers, but maybe this was just another romantic pipe dream of Mark's and he'd get over it.

"No building until I get home, promise?" she said.

"Yeah sure, Lou," he said, but the wistful glint was still in his eye. He'd caught some kind of dream, maybe from the silver light glinting off the mirrored windows of the trailer, maybe from the pattern the blue shadows made, racing over the flat lands.

Louise shrugged. She was pretty sure the whole thing was his idea and Janet would never be caught dead moving out here — Janet and her fake crab salad and her many cats. If they ever moved, Janet would have to have a house she could show off — maybe with fake pine panelling and a fake fireplace with plastic logs. Maybe she could grow plastic flowers in her garden.

"Oh shut up," Louise thought to herself. "You're getting bitter and old and mean." She started to turn away from Mark, then caught herself and turned back.

"Mark," she said,"I been talking to George. He thinks I should plant a new orchard here, peaches and apricots and grapes."

"Jeez, Lou, I don't know." Mark's boot toe scuffed the dirt. "A hell of a lot of work and not much money in it ..."

"Yeah, I know," she said.

"But it'd be nice to see the old place productive again. It ought to pay for itself somehow. It's good land. We both know that. Shit, the old man could grow anything, eh?"

"Yeah, and the trees we got are getting old."

"Yeah, well, let me know. Sounds good, I guess. You know a lot more about that stuff than I do. You always were the farmer in the family. Me, I could never get into it. You know, I used to be so jealous of you and the old man. You had that to share. Me, I never knew what you two were talking about, half the time."

When they said goodbye, they hugged each other hard and fierce and fast and then she walked away to the trailer, her back stiff. Mark stared after her before hoisting himself into his silver diesel four-by-four and grinding carefully out of the yard.

On the last day, Louise loaded her truck by herself. She hadn't wanted any help, although Celeste and Harold had offered. The whole thing was too much to take in. She wanted — she needed — to move at her own crabby careful pace, handling the bits and pieces of her life like bits of old crystal, mourning or rejoicing at things she might take, things she couldn't. She hadn't really known what to take; she hadn't known how to take apart her life for this adventure.

When she had left Stephen, she had left everything behind, glad to be rid of it. She would have walked out of his house naked, if she could have. It was he who finally packed her clothes and the things he considered hers, in an awkwardly selfish division of property. He kept their fine new stereo, but gave her the small cassette deck that had always sat on the kitchen counter. He brought a couple of plants which he hadn't bothered to water and which, despite Louise's nursing, finally died. He brought some blankets and towels, and a box of dishes and pots and silverware. He left them in Louise's kitchen when she wasn't home.

She thought about that now, while packing. It was another little bitter stroke against him. What an arrogant thing to do — to bring her enough bits of her shattered life to let her go on surviving, but not surviving too well, not too comfortably. She hadn't seen it then. She had actually thought he was being thoughtful. She had thought she ought to feel grateful.

This time, she took a bit of everything: a mattress, her clothes, some books, some blankets, her favourite purple pillow, even camping gear. If the truck died, she thought, she'd just settle down and live beside the road somewhere. She took as much as she could of the real food from the garden, knowing it wouldn't last a week before it rotted, and left the rest for the bears or Celeste or Marie — whoever got there first. She kept herself moving, though she had to stop every little while and stare over the valley and wait for the clenched fist in her stomach to stop hammering at her spine. It bent her over, unable to breathe.

Becky drove into the yard at noon.

"I picked up some mail for you." She had an odd expression on her face. Louise looked at her. Becky never could keep a secret. "Mail?" Louise said, stupidly. Then, numbly, she held out her hand.

The note from Susan was on dull purple paper, scented with lavender — lovely, textured, recycled paper. Of course, it would be.

"You told her I was moving," she said bitterly to Becky.

"No, I didn't," she protested. "Well, yeah, someone at the university must have. I didn't even know she worked there. Well, I sort of did. But it wasn't me told her. C'mon, at least read the goddamn letter. Quit bitching at me."

"I heard from the registrar," the letter read, "who's a friend of mine, that you were coming here to go to school. That's great. I know tons of people who will be so glad to meet you. Here's my phone number and address, if you want to call or stop by. Looking forward to seeing you again. Love, Susan."

"Oh no," said Louise, feeling sick and weak at the knees. "Just like that, she expects me to visit — like we're just friends, like nothing ever happened. How the hell does she expect me to do that?"

Becky carefully didn't say anything.

Louise threw a last box on the truck, fetched a coil of yellow rope and a tarpaulin and began the complicated process of tying down the tarp so it wouldn't flap in the wind and drive her crazy with the noise, or let in the rain or let things fly out. She had to tie and untie and retie the ropes three times until they were as tight as she could make them. Then she had to climb back inside under the tarp because she figured it might be better to have her tent on the outside where she could reach it in case she wanted to stop for the night.

Becky stood watching and didn't offer to help.

Louise jumped down off the truck.

"I don't understand," she snarled at Becky. "I just don't get it. How could she do this? Write me a nice little normal letter, like we're friends, like we could just pick up somehow, and pretend nothing had ever happened." Her voice choked. She turned away.

"That woman," she said, biting into the words like they were sour green apples, "that goddamn woman ripped my life to shreds. She goddamn near finished me off. And now I've picked up all the pieces and started over again and she blows in like a goddamn north wind. For what? To finish me off for good?"

She stomped inside the trailer without inviting Becky in, but Becky followed and sat in the only chair left in the place while Louise went back out, found a pot, found teabags, came in, boiled water and made tea, each movement deliberate and careful.

All the while, voices blew cold and shrill in her brain — arguments coming from all sides, trying to make sense, trying to understand what this meant ... that Susan considered her a "friend," could write her a cheerful letter offering to introduce her to "friends." Was this how it happened? Was she expected to be this casual? Could she be? Was this her mistake, that she had taken everything too seriously all along and consequently mistaken Susan's intentions?

"So, is that it, Beck? Have I just been stupid and naive all along? Just never get it, do I? Never know the rules, never figure out the goddamn game, isn't that what you said? Never get on the inside with the real people — just sit out here in the woods, thinking my life is something I own, something I can make my own goddamn rules for … Fuck it, Becky. That's it. To hell with them all." She slammed the teapot down hard on the counter and it shattered into bright brown shards of glass. Tea leaves and tea slid over the side of the counter and pooled on the floor. Becky and Louise stared at it. Becky shrugged, stood up and went outside.

Louise watched the tea run in a fine misty trickle off the counter. Shards of brown pottery littered the carpet. She left the whole mess dripping and went back outside. Becky had gone off to fetch wood from the shed; when she came back, she made a fire and rolled them both cigarettes. Silently, Louise went to the truck, fished out an old aluminum saucepan and made more tea over the fire. Then they sat on the dusty yellow August grass and watched the first bright star come into the dark-blue evening sky.

"I'll figure it out, Beck," she said. "I'll figure it out, all of it, all the rules and all the games. And then I'll come back and I won't have to care anymore because it won't matter. It probably never has but at least I'll know that. I'll still have this place and my life and they can have their games. I'll figure it out and then I'll go back to pruning trees and to hell with them."

"Guess I'll have to get some more new clothes," she added, after a while, just a little bitterly. "Maybe some of those fancy boots."

"Wear your logging boots. You'll be a big hit."

"Yeah, and my red plaid jacket. Maybe I'll take my pruning shears and go down to the goddamn park and give it a haircut. That'd be a big hit too. Maybe I'll get Mark to show up with his goddamn chain saw and we'll really give the place a haircut. Now wouldn't that get us a little attention?"

"If that's what you want," said Becky. She wasn't laughing anymore.

"You know," she added, "I'm really going to miss you. Make sure you come back, eh? Won't be much fun any more around here without you." Her voice was wistful.

"Yeah, you've still got Luke."

"Yeah, I do, and I want you around too." She shifted over and put her arms around Louise and they held each other for a long time.

"Do good, kid. Do good for all of us."

When Becky left, it was dark. The wind coming down the mountain had a bite in it. Louise shivered and fetched a jacket, and then stood under the old Gravenstein — her favourite tree — looking over the valley and the mountains. The lazy brown river was hazing to black in the evening light and the thunderheads, shot through with purple and gold lights, were piling up on the mountains.

"I love you," she said. "I've always loved you. I always will."

She waited, standing in the silence, until it was too dark to see; and then she undid the tarpaulin, pulled her mattress off the back of the truck, lay down beside the fire and watched it burn until there were only tiny sparks, like the lights of a strange, bright, distant city, to keep her company while she slept.

The Best of gynergy books

The Harriet Hubbley Mystery Series, *Jackie Manthorne.* The Harriet Hubbley Series features gripping mysteries with a lesbian twist and a dash of sly humour. "Manthorne knows how to keep the action moving." *The Globe and Mail*
Ghost Motel ISBN 0-921881-31-2 $9.95
Deadly Reunion ISBN 0-921881-32-0 $10.95
Last Resort ISBN 0-921881-34-7 $10.95

By Word of Mouth: Lesbians Write the Erotic, *Lee Fleming (ed.).* "Contains plenty of sexy good writing and furthers the desperately needed honest discussion of what we mean by 'erotic' and by 'lesbian.'" *Sinister Wisdom*
ISBN 0-921881-06-1 $10.95/$12.95 U.S.

Lesbian Parenting: Living with Pride & Prejudice, *Katherine Arnup (ed.).* Here is the perfect primer for lesbian parents, and a helpful resource for their families and friends. "Thoughtful, provocative and passionate. A brave and necessary book." *Sandra Butler*
ISBN 0-921881-33-9 $19.95/$16.95 U.S.

To Sappho, My Sister: Lesbian Sisters Write About Their Lives, *Lee Fleming (ed.).* This one-of-a-kind anthology includes the stories of both well-known and less famous siblings from three continents, in a compelling portrait of lesbian sisterhood.
ISBN 0-921881-36-3 $16.95/$14.95 U.S.

Triad Moon, *Gillean Chase.* Meet Lila, Brook and Helen, three women whose bonds of love take them beyond conventional relationships. *Triad Moon* is an exhilarating read that skilfully explores past and present lives, survival from incest, and healing.
ISBN 0-921881-28-2 $9.95

Woman in the Rock, *Claudia Gahlinger.* A haunting collection of stories about forgetting and remembering incest, by an award-winning author. Gahlinger's characters live near the sea and find consolation in fishing, an act that allows for the eventual emergence of the "woman in the rock."
ISBN 0-921881-26-6 $10.95/$9.95 U.S.

gynergy books titles are available at quality bookstores. Ask for our titles at your favourite local bookstore. Individual, prepaid orders may be sent to: **gynergy books,** P.O. Box 2023, Charlottetown, Prince Edward Island, Canada, C1A 7N7. Please add postage and handling ($3 for the first book and 75 cents for each additional book) to your order. Canadian residents add 7% GST to the total amount. GST registration number R104383120. Prices are subject to change without notice.